ORACLE PROJECT

IN MY MIND'S EYE™
BOOK ONE

KELLI ROBYNS

MICHAEL ANDERLE

DON'T MISS OUR NEW RELEASES

Join the Florid Romance email list to be notified of new releases and special promotions (which happen often) by following this link:

https://floridromance.lmbpn.com/about/sign-up-for-our-newsletter/

Published by Florid Romance
an imprint of LMBPN Publishing
2375 E. Tropicana Avenue, Suite 8-305
Las Vegas, Nevada 89119 USA

Version 1.00, August 2025
eBook ISBN: 979-8-89354-945-4
Print ISBN: 979-8-89354-946-1

ONE

THE VISION

Ivy Lewis woke with a jolt. Her pulse pounded against her rib cage as she stared through the early-morning darkness. She sucked in a frantic breath, half expecting to smell the stale, oily air of an underground train station, thick with the metallic tang of the rails and the damp humidity of mud on concrete. For a moment, her mind scrambled. Where was she? The screech of a subway car lingered in her ears, the phantom echo of metal-on-metal clinging to her thoughts like a burr. She stretched out a hand, fumbling for the bedside lamp. A soft glow lit the contours of her small bedroom, revealing the lines of her worn wooden dresser and the rust-colored quilt folded at the foot of the bed. She exhaled, trying to retreat from the vividness of the nightmare.

She swept a damp curl of hair away from her forehead. "It was just a dream," she whispered, but the tremble in her voice gave away how real it had felt. The images rushed through her mind in rapid bursts. A man in a red scarf stood too close to the edge of a train platform, the shrill warning bell ringing out with a piercing, insistent rhythm. Then a sudden shift, the blur of the scarf as he fell, and a hollow thud that made Ivy's stomach turn even as she was awake. She closed her eyes, firmly pressing her fingertips to her temples. The memory clung to her like a heavy cloak. The buzzing fluorescent lights cast a sickly yellow pallor on everything, the slick, grimy platform of the subway station, the honk of a distant train speeding on its tracks.

She inhaled slowly. Outside her bedroom window, the faintest trace of dawn tinted the clouds in hues of gray and purple. San Francisco always stirred early, even on mornings when the fog hugged the city's rooftops. She could already hear a distant rumble of traffic, a gritty hum that grounded her, though it also reminded her too much of the train's screech. Ivy threw off her quilt and swung her legs over the side of the bed. Her reflection in the mirror across the room revealed wide, anxious eyes. She blinked, half expecting to see that red scarf behind her in the glass. Of course, there was nothing but the reflection of her own face and the wooden headboard.

She reached for her phone. The screen displayed 5:45 a.m. She usually opened her little shop, The Oracle, around ten, but she knew she would not be falling back asleep after a dream like that. The idea of lying in bed with the scenario replaying on a loop made her stomach twist. She decided to get up, make coffee, and journal the scene before it slipped from her memory. Over the last few months, she had recorded many odd dreams and half-visions in a spiral notebook. Most, she could wave off as whimsical, like a flock of birds spelling out a word in the sky or conversations with mysterious shrouded figures who spoke in riddles. This one felt disturbingly tangible, grounded in a reality she could not ignore.

The layout of her small apartment forced her to walk barely a dozen steps from her bed to the tiny kitchenette. She filled the kettle, then prepared her French press. While waiting, she wandered into the living room, running a finger along the windowsill. The window faced the street, the lingering darkness outside revealing no more than the vague silhouette of a car parked outside. The dream replayed in her head. The red scarf. The slick platform. The heavy sound of impact. She felt breathless just thinking about it.

A soft whistle from the kettle brought her back. As she poured the water, she drew another deep breath and tried to steady herself. Maybe someone had left a TV on overnight, and random sounds had seeped into her dream. She tried to rationalize, though her heart had yet to slow. Once she had her coffee, she carried it to a small desk in the corner of her living room. She flipped open the spiral notebook and uncapped a pen with a shaky hand, writing down fragments in uneven handwriting.

Subway car screech. Red scarf. 2 a.m. vibe? Man falling. Yellow umbrella. Body hits rails. Oil smell. The sound of a bell somewhere in the distance.

She paused, tapping the pen against the margin. The yellow umbrella. Why had that detail surfaced? Flashes of the dream re-emerged. She had glimpsed a bright yellow umbrella floating through the bustling station, as though belonging to someone walking on the adjacent platform. It was a jarring splash of color in an otherwise gray and menacing scene. Ivy wrote that down too, then shut the notebook. "It means nothing," she murmured, though a heavy weight in her chest conveyed otherwise. At close to seven, the sky lightened, the clouds overhead taking on a milky hue. Ivy sipped the last of her coffee and got ready for the day. She threw on a soft sweater and a pair of comfortable jeans, letting her dark curls tumble over her shoulders. A brisk walk to The Oracle might chase away the lingering dread.

Outside, the air carried a typical San Francisco chill, brisk and damp. She tucked her hands into her pockets. A distant bus rumbled past, a large advertisement plastered on its side. She stared a second too long at the image of a smiling actor wearing a bright red scarf. Her breath caught, and she turned away, picking up her pace. "Coincidence," she told herself sharply, refusing to let a random ad spark more panic.

The Oracle was housed in a narrow storefront with bay windows. Painted tarot cards adorned the glass, chipped by years of salty fog. As she opened the door, the familiar scent of incense and candle wax greeted her. The place was quiet, exactly as it had been when she had closed the evening before. She switched on the lights, revealing a wooden counter, a few plush chairs, and the small round table where she gave readings. Though her personal faith in magic remained uncertain most days, she had a knack for reading people's energies. Her friend Robin often joked that Ivy's real skill was empathy, not prophecy.

She stood in the center of the shop, inhaling the faint trace of lavender in the air. As her mind strayed again to the dream's intensity, she shoved the memory away. She had a routine to maintain. She placed a few fresh candles around the room and retrieved her favorite deck of tarot cards from behind the counter. The gilded edges always comforted her, a reminder that despite the unknown, there was artistry and beauty in interpretation.

Half an hour later, the sun started to burn through the haze, casting watery light onto the sidewalk. Ivy decided to do a personal reading to calm herself. She lit a candle, whispered a small grounding prayer, and shuffled the tarot deck. She laid her palm on top, closing her eyes to focus. Today, she wanted reassurance. She drew three cards and placed them face-down on the table. When she flipped the first one, her stomach twisted. The Tower. A tall spire struck by lightning, figures tumbling from its high windows. Her breath hitched. In her experience, The Tower never meant a minor inconvenience. It was always a harbinger of foundational collapse, of truths revealed through destruction.

"Just a coincidence," she muttered under her breath. She flipped the second card. The Eight of Swords. A blindfolded figure ringed by blades. A card of powerlessness, of being trapped by one's own perceptions. Ivy forced a small, hollow laugh. She pressed her palm against her chest, searching for calm. The final card she turned over was the Page of Cups reversed, which she typically associated with an emotional imbalance or a warning to listen to intuition. She brushed her fingertips lightly over the illustrations. In isolation, these cards were not disastrous, but in her current state, they felt too unsettling to brush aside.

She scooped them up and returned them to the deck. The dream hammered at her mind again. The red scarf, the jarring fall, everything that followed. She wondered if she should call the police, but the notion sounded absurd. She pictured an officer's baffled expression if she lodged a complaint saying, "I had a dream about a man falling on the train tracks, and it felt real." They would likely dismiss her. She paced behind the counter, unconsciously chewing the edge of her thumbnail.

As the city fully woke, a few pedestrians passed the storefront. One woman held a bright yellow umbrella. Ivy froze. It was the exact color from her nightmare. Her pulse surged, yet she tried to remain calm. San Francisco had thousands of umbrellas. She forced her gaze away and busied herself straightening a display of crystal pendants near the cash register.

The day crept by slowly. Only two customers wandered in. One was a wide-eyed college student asking for a reading on her love life, and the other was an older woman seeking something for anxiety. Ivy performed both sessions politely, but her usual warmth faltered. She felt as if she were moving underwater, half there and half lost in the gloom of her dream. In the moments between customers, she found herself staring into nothing, anticipating the echo of an oncoming train.

By mid-afternoon, a heavier fog rolled in, and business lulled to silence. Ivy slumped in the rickety chair behind the counter, massaging her temples. A headache pulsed, made worse by the flare of candles she had forgotten to extinguish. She blew them out one by one, inhaling the faint ribbons of smoke. She decided to close early. She told herself it was just a slow day, but privately she admitted she could not bear more forced smiles or constant watchfulness for red scarves and yellow umbrellas.

Before locking up, she pressed her forehead against the glass door and looked out. Cars rolled by. The city itself felt indifferent, continuing to breathe and churn as it always did. Yet Ivy could not shake the feeling that something dangerous lurked beneath the surface. Something real.

She flipped the sign on the door to CLOSED and drew the blinds. The gentle clink of metal against glass calmed her a little, giving her a sense of separation from the outside world. She retreated to the back room, grabbing her bag and slipping her tarot deck inside. Soon, she reminded herself, she would be home to the comforting hum of her kettle and the mindless background noise of a radio. The dream would fade with the day. When she finally stepped onto the sidewalk and locked the storefront, the air felt colder. She cradled her keys in her hand, hesitating. Though it was still afternoon, the streetlights shone ghostly in the fog. An odd sense of deja vu crept over her. In the distance, she heard a train horn, faint but unmistakable, reminding her that the city's transit lines never truly slept.

Block by block, she walked home. The dream's intensity refused to quiet. Stray images teased her peripheral vision. A poster in a café window echoed the shape of a train. A reflective puddle gave off an oily sheen reminiscent of the station floor. Each sight tugged at her nerves. By the time she reached her apartment building, her shoulders were tight, and her breath shallow. She let herself in, flipping the lock behind her. The hallway smelled of someone's curry dinner, a comforting reminder of mundane life. Inside her apartment, she sank onto the couch, dropping her bag at her feet. The quiet pressed in. She stared at the blank television screen, afraid to turn it on and learn of real tragedies. If she discovered that her dream had roots in reality, she was not sure how she would react.

She set her phone on the coffee table, letting it vibrate with an incoming notification. She would deal with calls and messages later. She tugged a knitted throw over her lap, feeling the day's tension settle in her muscles. The memory of the dream refused to vanish, yet exhaustion weighed her down more strongly. Leaning her head against the cushion, she let her eyes close. The last wave of twilight slipped through her curtains. In her living room, she could still smell iron and concrete, still hear the subterranean scream of a train's brakes. "It was just a dream," she whispered, voice as soft as the fog that blanketed the city. She did not fully believe it.

Tomorrow, she might wake ready to dismiss every eerie sign. Or she might wake more certain that her mind was telling her something she could not afford to ignore. For now, she simply sank into uneasy sleep, the image of a crimson scarf breathing down her neck.

TWO

THE REPORT

Ivy lingered across the street from the squat, gray-stone police station, her spiral notebook clutched in clammy hands. The midmorning sun glinted off rows of parked squad cars. She told herself a single line over and over. "You're not crazy." Her pulse thrummed in her ears, a frantic drumbeat against the city's hum. She remembered a time, years ago, when she had tried to tell her mother about a vision of a neighbor's car accident just moments before it happened. Her mother had denied her, her eyes wide with a fear that looked almost like anger.

Don't say such things, Ivy. People will think you're strange.

The memory was a ghost at her shoulder, whispering doubt. She forced her feet to move, crossing the street and pushing through the station's heavy doors. The placard to her left read SFPD in dull metal letters, as if to confirm she could still turn around if she wanted to. She slipped inside, fists clenched so tight that her knuckles paled.

A stale odor filled the waiting area, thick with the

sharp smell of antiseptic and old coffee. A woman in a crisp blazer murmured instructions to a man filling out forms at a narrow counter. Ivy cleared her throat and approached a tall, curved desk manned by a uniformed officer who glanced up from his computer.

He offered a polite, practiced smile. "May I help you?"

She managed a nod. "I...yes. I want to report something. A crime, maybe. Or maybe it's about to be." The words tumbled out in a breathy rush. "I'm not sure what to call it." The officer's smile wavered. He motioned for her to continue. Ivy lifted her notebook and held it close to her chest. The edges of the paper had curled from the dampness of her grip.

"I had a dream. No, it was more like a premonition. A man fell from the BART platform. He was wearing a red scarf, and he was right at the edge when the train came." Her throat went dry. "It was so vivid, I thought I should report it."

For a moment, the officer simply blinked. The station hallway seemed thicker now. A pair of on-duty policemen strode by, talking about a stolen car, barely glancing at her. She drew a shaky breath and plunged on.

"I saw him hit the tracks," she continued, tapping her notebook with a trembling finger. "It felt real, like I was actually there. The station in my dream looked like Powell Street, maybe. It was a BART station downtown. I believe it was in the early hours of the morning. I can't say exactly."

Her cheeks burned. She braced for laughter, but the officer only pressed his lips into a line. "Ma'am, can you clarify whether a crime took place or if this is something you suspect might happen?"

"I'm concerned it either happened overnight or it will happen soon." He nodded slowly, then glanced at his computer.

"Your name?"

"Ivy Lewis."

He typed. Air hissed from a nearby vent, and Ivy noticed her reflection glistening on the polished counter. She looked pale, her eyes shadowed. *This is ridiculous*, she thought. *No one believes in psychic dreams. Why am I here?*

While she wrestled with self-consciousness, the officer cleared his throat. "I'll see if there's any report of someone falling on the tracks last night or early this morning." He lifted a phone receiver and dialed a short number. "Dispatcher, any accidents at the BART stations matching..." He glanced at Ivy. "Someone in a red scarf?"

Ivy curled her arms around her midsection, wishing she could vanish. Her insides twisted when he shook his head at the answer coming through the phone. He ended the call with a polite, "Thanks." When he set the receiver down, his expression grew more sympathetic.

"I'm sorry, Miss Lewis, but there are no reports matching your description. Not from any station in the city."

She pressed her notebook tighter against her chest. "Are you certain?" The question came out in a desperate whisper. "Maybe they just dismissed it. Or, maybe, someone else would have reported it?" She realized she was babbling and stopped.

His voice softened. "Miss Lewis, I appreciate your concern, but the station managers log any incidents, especially one as major as a person falling onto the tracks. There's nothing like that in the logs."

A wave of embarrassment rolled through her, but also relief. If her dream had not happened, no one was hurt. So why did her heart squeeze painfully? She swallowed. "Okay, thanks for checking. Could you at least keep a note, in case something like that gets reported soon? It's possible it hasn't happened yet."

The officer's brow furrowed. He released a careful sigh. "I can make a note that you were here, Miss Lewis. But truthfully, we might classify this under suspicious activity or mental health concerns if there's no direct evidence."

The suggestion flared hot in her ears. "I'm not hallucinating," she maintained, voice shaking. "I know how this sounds, but someone should be careful near the BART platforms, especially if he's wearing..."

"Miss Lewis," the officer interrupted gently. "If I may ask, are you on any medication, or have you been under stress?"

She glimpsed movement in the waiting area. A man sat on a wooden bench, scrolling on his phone and sipping from a to-go coffee cup. He was tall, dressed in a rumpled button-down. Something about the way he watched them made a flush creep up Ivy's neck. He was not just glancing over. His focus was sharp, his posture alert. She snapped her gaze back to the officer.

"I'm fine," she said, forcing each syllable evenly. "No medication, just worried."

The officer spread his hands. "I can't pursue an investigation of a dream, ma'am. If you see something or hear something more concrete, please let us know immediately." He sounded weary now. "For now, it might be best if you talk to a friend or a counselor. Stress can do weird things."

Ivy's eyes burned, but she refused to cry. She cleared her throat and shoved the notebook into her bag. "Right. I understand."

He stood from behind the desk and guided her toward the door. As they passed the bench, she noticed the man watching from under his dark hair. He lowered his phone slightly, his gaze narrowed with a sharp curiosity.

"Did you get any help?" he asked, his tone neutral. Before Ivy could reply, the officer pressed her forward.

"This way, please."

Outside, the sky seemed too bright, and the midday heat made her dizzy. The officer paused at the top of the steps, sympathy plain in his eyes. "Please stay safe. If you need a friend or a family member to come get you, let me know."

She mustered a forced smile. "I'll be all right."

He nodded and returned inside. Ivy stayed on the steps, balancing between humiliation and persistent dread. She closed her eyes. The memory hit her again. Shrieking brakes, a flash of red fabric, the horrible impact. "I'm not crazy," she whispered once more. When she reached the sidewalk, she realized her palms were damp. She tightened her bag's strap, uncertain what to do next. She turned right, intending to walk back to The Oracle. As she passed a small convenience store, she caught her reflection in the window. She hated how lost she looked

Her phone buzzed in her bag, but she could not bring herself to check it. She was too drained to talk to anyone, even a friend. She stepped off the curb, picking up her pace when she realized she had to cross an intersection before the signal changed. A few heartbeats later, she glanced over her shoulder. The man with the coffee, the one who had watched her inside, stepped from the station. He paused on the sidewalk, phone in one hand, gaze scanning the street. The sun caught the faintest gold glints in his eyes. An uneasy feeling twitched in her stomach.

She told herself not to worry, but her heart pounded faster. Gripping her bag strap, she continued forward, weaving through pedestrians who jostled in conversation. She tried to breathe slowly. The bus stop two blocks ahead offered a bench, but she was not sure if she wanted to sit. She only knew she wanted to be far from the station, from that officer's pitying expression. Behind her, a car engine turned over. She caught a glimpse of the man sliding into a modest sedan. He placed his coffee in the cup holder and checked his side mirror. Her pulse spiked. He could not be following her. Perhaps he was just leaving in the same direction. She tried to lose him, ducking into a small bakery with a window full of poppy seed rolls. Pretending to study the pastries, she watched his sedan crawl past. He slowed, his head turning, scanning the storefronts. He was looking for her.

Casting one more nervous glance behind her, she willed her legs to keep moving out the other side of the bakery. The day stretched hot and disorienting. She replayed the policeman's words in her mind. Maybe I imagined it, she thought. But as she retraced the dream's images, oil-slick rails, the clang of an approaching train, her gut insisted it was more than fantasy. When she reached the bus stop, she paused. The next vehicle was not due for several minutes, and a teenage boy with earphones sat scowling silently on the bench. Ivy stared at the route map and tried to focus on her next steps. She thought about calling her best friend, Robin, but decided she needed air and time to compose herself first. She would just walk.

The presence of the sedan a few yards behind her put her nerves on edge again. It stayed a few yards behind her. Struggling not to look obvious, she risked a sideways peek. The same man again, window lowered, his gaze lifting from his phone to trace her figure. He did not appear hostile, but a sharp curiosity burned in his eyes.

She had never met him before, that was certain. Yet something about him felt almost familiar, the way a stranger might show up in a dream. She forced herself to step away from the bus stop, crossing the next crosswalk with brisk strides. Her thoughts swirled. *Did he overhear what I said? Does he think I'm delusional?* She passed a row of small shops. A florist with a riot of orchids in the window. A half-closed bookstore that smelled of warmth and old pages. A flutter from the corner of her vision warned her that the sedan had turned the corner after her. The man sped ahead slightly, as if trying to keep her in his peripheral view. Ivy's heart thudded so loudly she felt her eardrums tense.

When she neared a side alley, she debated slipping through it but immediately dismissed the idea as reckless. Instead, she continued along the main road. *Why follow me?* She saw the next intersection up ahead, where she would turn for the quick route back to The Oracle. *Perhaps he was only heading the same way or searching for a parking space.* She reassured herself, hoping it would slow her frantic breathing.

Traffic crawled, so she made faster progress on foot. With every few steps, she sensed his presence, as if he were hovering just within her line of sight. When she reached the next crosswalk, she paused at the red light. The sedan rolled closer. She dared another glance and locked eyes with him for one tense moment. He tilted his head, and his mouth quirked as if he might say something if he could. But the line of cars forced him to keep moving.

The light turned green, and she crossed quickly. The sidewalk seemed narrower now, lined by high brick buildings on either side. The city noises pressed around her, and she fought the urge to cover her ears. By the time she arrived at the corner with a gleaming streetlamp, she could still see the sedan, engine idling at a stop sign. The man inside tapped his fingers on the steering wheel as though debating whether to continue. Two teenage girls walked by with iced coffees, oblivious to Ivy's racing thoughts. Her steps slowed. She realized the man was, indeed, following her. If he intended danger, she saw no immediate escape. She swallowed hard. She had never intended for this day to spiral out of control.

Finally, she turned down a quieter street, leading toward her shop and the small apartment above it. A pang of relief hit her when she realized the sedan could not follow her onto this one-way lane without circling the block. She glanced over her shoulder and saw him watch her, phone lifted as if making notes or taking a photo. Then he drove on, merging into traffic and disappearing.

Ivy's hand shook when she pressed it to her chest. "You're fine," she whispered. "He's gone." Still, her veins thrummed with anxiety. Something about the way that man had looked at her gave her the strangest certainty that this was not over. She had felt an uncanny intensity in his gaze, not predatory but searching, as though he had recognized something in her. For a long moment, she stood on the sidewalk, trying to gather the courage to walk the final two blocks to The Oracle. A small breeze kicked up, ruffling her hair. She needed a mug of tea, a quiet corner, and something to calm her churning mind. Shaking off her fear, she continued toward her shop.

Behind her, in the slow tangle of traffic, Ethan Matson's sedan glided into a side street. He eased behind a parked car and switched off his headlights. He took a final sip of burnt coffee and set the cup aside. He scribbled a note in his leather-bound notebook.

Ivy Lewis. BART accident claim. Powell St. Red

scarf. Dismissed by SFPD. Possibly sees things. Investigate further.

A curious spark lit his eyes. He started the engine and edged forward, intent on staying close enough to see where she went without alarming her. He had come that morning to chase another lead, but now he found himself intrigued by the haunted look on her face and the conviction with which she had spoken. She did not seem deranged or hysterical. She looked like a person weighed down by something she believed was real.

Ethan smiled. He had a feeling Ivy Lewis would be more than a mere footnote in his story. If she had glimpsed something, even if it was only a hunch, it was enough to pique his reporter's instincts. He would find out what secrets she truly possessed.

CHAPTER

THREE

THE INTERVIEW

Ivy leaned her shoulder against the shop's glass door, laptop bag still pressed to her side. She had walked the few blocks from the police station with her mind swimming. Her pulse, although calmer, still thrummed with leftover unease. She had caught a glimpse of a car slipping into a slow crawl farther down the block. She told herself it could be anyone. Unwilling to feed her own paranoia, she focused on unlocking the door to The Oracle.

A narrow hallway led into the shop, its windows decorated with hand-painted tarot card motifs. The Moon, The High Priestess, and a whimsical spiral that Robin had once insisted signified "mystic vibes." Ivy gazed at them fondly. This small, cozy space was a sanctuary of sorts. She opened the door fully, switched the CLOSED sign to OPEN, and turned the overhead lights on. Inside came that familiar scent of leftover incense and the lemony note of furniture polish. It made her feel momentarily safe.

She set her phone beside the cash register, trying to ignore the flutter of anxiety. The station visit had not gone as she hoped. Her dream had earned only polite dismissal. The man with the coffee had watched her, and she had felt his stare. Maybe she had imagined it, but part of her suspected he was the same person in that slow-moving sedan.

She exhaled, brushing away the thought and turned to straighten the small round table where she gave her readings. The tablecloth, patterned with faint stars, needed a shake. She lifted a small candle from the edge of the table and placed it onto a mirrored tray. Her tarot decks rested neatly in a wooden box. She touched them lightly, half tempted to do a quick spread for herself, but her nerves felt too frazzled.

As she was debating whether she ought to slip into the back kitchen for tea, a distinct rumble sounded outside. Through the window's painted cards, she saw a sedan parking by the curb. The door opened, and a man in a loose-fitting hat stepped out. It was hard to see his face with the brim pulled low, but something about his posture struck a chord in Ivy's memory. She recognized the crisp line of his jaw when he lifted his head. Her stomach tensed.

She forced herself to stand tall. If he came in, she decided, she would be polite, nothing more. The timid squeak of the door opening followed, and then the delicate chime from the small bell overhead.

"Hello," she called quietly, hearing the unsteadiness in her own voice. "Come in."

The man stepped forward. He wore a plain T-shirt that looked freshly changed. His gaze took in the shelves of crystals and stacked books, then turned to meet her eyes. Ivy recognized him at once. He was the one who had watched her in the station lobby, coffee cup balanced on his knee. There was no coffee cup now, but the intensity in his stare was the same. Dark hair, faint stubble, and a calm near-smile that made her impatient.

"Can I help you?" she asked, voice polite.

He gestured to the sign overhead where gold letters spelled The Oracle. "I was hoping to get a reading. I heard you were... insightful." His tone was casual, yet something about it told Ivy he was sifting for details.

"We offer tarot readings here," she replied. For a moment, she wished Robin were around to cut through the tension. "If that's what you're looking for."

He nodded once. "Yes. A reading sounds good."

Ivy folded her arms. She had offered many readings to curious tourists and local skeptics. Usually they came in groups, giggling about fortunes. This was different. She remembered how he had listened while she spoke to the officer, how his brow had furrowed. A slow unease spread through her, but she gestured to the round table all the same. "Have a seat."

He thanked her and sank into the chair. She moved to the table's opposite side. The overhead light caught his eyes for a second, and she noticed an odd gold fleck in his irises. It shimmered when he blinked.

She cleared her throat. "Name?"

He shrugged. "Ethan."

She hoped for a last name. He gave none, so she let it drop. "All right, Ethan. Is there anything specific on your mind?"

He lifted a shoulder, leaning back in his chair. "I feel uncertain about the future."

Ivy smiled without warmth. "Aren't we all?" She reached for her gilded deck, cradling it gently. "I'll shuffle, you'll cut the cards. Easy enough."

She shuffled, aware that his gaze never left her face. Despite the pang of anxiety that told her he was here for more than just a friendly tarot session, she forced herself to proceed as she would with any client. She placed the deck before him. "Cut them once."

He complied, though the quickness of his movement suggested impatience. His hand brushed hers as he passed the deck back. A faint static prickle lit her palm. She drew in a breath and laid out three cards. The first card she flipped over made her mouth tighten. The Tower. A tall spire struck by lightning, figures tumbling from its heights, signaling upheaval, sudden change, or truths forcibly revealed. She raised her eyes to Ethan, but he offered no reaction.

She turned the second card. The Eight of Swords. It depicted a blindfolded figure surrounded by blades, a sense of self-imposed restriction. Ivy's stomach twisted. The final card startled her. It was from a deck variant that labeled a figure simply The Watcher of Flames. A man in a cloak stood near a crackling fire, head bowed as though searching for answers in the embers. She had often interpreted it as a synergy of intuition and destructive potential, a confrontation with inner truths, or hidden motives about to be exposed.

Ethan looked at the three images without surprise. Ivy shifted in her seat. "This is a... compelling combination," she commented, voice subdued. "The Tower suggests a major disruption, something you might not be ready for. The Eight of Swords indicates entrapment or denial. And The Watcher of Flames is about facing what you fear might burn away your illusions." She paused. "Put plainly, you've either been lying to yourself or to me."

A flash of amusement lit his features. "That's an interesting claim." He tapped a knuckle against The Tower's artwork.

Ivy's cheeks warmed. "Tarot isn't about me guessing your secrets," she retorted measuredly. "It's a mirror. It shows possibilities, not certainties. It draws out truths if you're willing to see them."

He leaned forward slightly, arms resting on the table's edge. "So did you or did you not see me earlier, at the police station?"

She stilled. "I saw someone with a coffee," she answered, voice tight. "I remember he was quite interested in what I was saying."

A corner of his mouth curved. "I was curious to hear your conversation about a... vision?"

She shrugged, feeling a prickle of defensiveness. "Sounds to me like you have your own reasons for being here, Ethan."

For a moment, he spoke nothing. They locked eyes, and she became acutely aware of the tension in her shoulders. There was something oddly captivating in the way he regarded her, confident and guarded all at once. She noticed how his T-shirt clung to his shoulders, how his dark hair could use a trim, how those odd gold flecks in his gaze reminded her of a cat's eyes catching light.

He broke the silence. "I suppose hearing you talk about a fatal train accident that no one else reported got my attention. Are you in the habit of predicting things that never happen?"

Anger surged up her spine, but she steadied herself. "That's out of line," she responded softly. "You don't know what I predicted or why."

He raised both hands as if in a truce, but she saw skepticism brimming in his expression. "So, about these cards... Does The Tower mean I should watch my back? Or is it telling me to move to a remote mountain so I don't get struck by lightning?"

She exhaled sharply. "It means that if you're lying, you might not be able to keep up the act. The Tower topples illusions. The Eight of Swords... is a reminder that sometimes we blindfold ourselves because we can't handle the truth. The Watcher of Flames..."

He glanced at that final card. "Let me guess. Fire reveals what's beneath?"

"In a sense. Or it consumes. Depends how you confront it."

A mocking hint curved his lips. "That's rich, coming from a woman who sells glimpses of fate for fifty bucks a session." He tapped the edge of the table. "After all, you monetize illusions too."

Her face heated. His words stung. A large part of her had always wrestled with whether her readings were genuine or just performance. "Is that what you think this is?" she asked. "One big illusion?"

He frowned, but he did not retract his remark. "I think you must be good at reading people," he observed quietly. "Maybe you see more than most. Or maybe you see only what you want to see."

"And you," she asked, forcing calm, "see what?"

He paused. "I see a woman whose eyes hold too many questions. It makes me wonder if she believes in her own craft."

A flush raced up her neck. The strangest part was, despite his abrasive front, she sensed he had not come solely to mock her. He wanted answers. *But about what?* She considered her words carefully. "If you want to find out what I believe, you could have asked me in a normal way," she replied, setting the cards aside. "Instead, you watched me at the station and followed me here."

"Like I said, you piqued my interest."

She tipped her chin up. "Then consider it piqued back, especially if your plan is to dig around for a story." She eyed him. "Am I your next news piece?"

An unreadable flash crossed his face, and he stood. "I told you, I was just curious."

Though his tone had cooled, she caught a pulse of tension in it. She also noticed how he avoided giving a firm denial. Her mind whirled with the possibilities of who he might be. A reporter, a skeptic out to prove her a fraud, or something else. She watched him pick up his hat, the muscles in his forearm shifting. The overhead light blinked as she tried to ignore the growing pressure in her chest.

She rose from her chair. "If you're finished, we can wrap up." She gestured at the reading fee posted on a small stand. "That's my rate."

His gaze shifted to the sign, and his mouth quirked wryly. Fishing out a few bills from his back pocket, he placed them on the table.

"Worth every penny." His tone dripped with a mix of sarcasm and reluctant respect. He shot one more glance at the cards. "Tower. Eight of Swords. A man staring into flames. Quite the spread."

"Indeed," she replied, voice curt. "Thank you for stopping by."

He gave a slight nod, turned, and reached for the door. The sound of the small bell rang again when he pushed it open. Right at the threshold, he hesitated, glancing back at her. For an instant, she thought he might say something else. Instead, he simply studied her as if memorizing her expression, then walked out. The door shut behind him.

Ivy stood there, heart pounding. She realized she was breathing faster than normal. Everything about that exchange left her rattled, from the pointed questions to the way he talked about illusions. He had not confirmed why he was truly there. She guessed he wanted a story, something to do with her dream at the station. But there had also been a hint of... something else in his eyes.

FOUR

THE ECHO

Ivy picked at the crust of her sandwich, trying to ignore the gnawing tension in her stomach. She sat alone at a small circular table in The Oracle, the tang of lemon polish in the air. The open sign glowed faintly in the front window, but so far, no one had come in for a reading. She counted that as a mercy. The last thing she wanted was forced small talk when her mind still churned over the unnerving events of the previous day.

She glanced at her phone. Nothing yet. The clock read 12:17 PM, and her appetite was nonexistent despite the half-eaten sandwich resting on waxy paper. The bread was going stale at the edges, but she could not bring herself to finish it. Her phone vibrated against the table, a small buzz that jolted her. Her pulse spiked. She reached for the device with clammy fingers, expecting another spam text or maybe a client's cancellation. The screen displayed a breaking news alert from one of the city's local outlets. She tapped the notification and felt a hot rush of dread crawl up her spine as she read the headline. "Man Dies on BART Tracks at Powell Street Station, Witnesses Report Red Scarf."

For a long moment, her brain refused to piece the words together. She blinked, hoping she had misread. But every syllable stared back at her with grim clarity. The same station she had named to the policeman. The same color scarf she had shakily described. She forced herself to open the article, ignoring how her hand trembled. The text beneath the headline was brief, describing how early that morning, a commuter on the platform noticed a figure at the very edge of the tracks, a man wearing a bright red scarf. Moments later, the BART train hurtled in, and the man tumbled forward. By the time authorities arrived, it was too late.

She pushed her sandwich away. It fell to the floor with a dull thud. Her mouth went dry, and panic coiled hot in her stomach. She read the words again, eyes skipping desperately through the short paragraphs. Police investigating possible causes. BART surveillance footage under review. Identity of the victim not yet released. Witness statements indicate the victim stood near the platform edge. Red scarf found at the scene.

It matched. It all matched. The dream she had recounted at the police station had become reality. She had walked into that station yesterday to warn them, to keep this from happening. Her breath hitched, and she pressed a fist to her chest, trying to steady the uneven rhythm of her heartbeat. Thoughts crowded her skull. The officer had eyed her with polite skepticism and told her they had no reports of such an accident. Then he had gently ushered her to the door, as if worried she might cause a scene. She stole a shaky breath, remembering how humiliating that felt and how certain she had been that the danger was real.

Now someone was dead.

She stumbled up from her chair. A dull ache burned behind her ribs. The phone still glared with the harsh black text of the article. She wondered if the policeman from yesterday was reading the exact same lines and recalling her words. Or perhaps he had forgotten her entirely, chalking her up as misguided or troubled. The notion made her sick with frustration and guilt.

She scrambled around the shop, half-dazed. She rested a hand on the wooden counter that displayed small clusters of crystals. The earthy scent of incense usually calmed her, but now it only reminded her that she and her tarot readings were never taken seriously. Her mind whirled. Could she have stopped it, had someone believed her?

Her phone buzzed again. Another news outlet had posted a follow-up, confirming the time of the incident around 5:45 AM. She scrolled feverishly, devouring every detail. She found a line from a brief interview with a witness. "He wobbled forward, like he lost his balance. Then he was gone. He had on this red scarf, so I saw it flutter." Ivy's lips parted in a silent gasp. The memory of her dream swept over her. The screech of brakes, the jolt of an approaching train, the final blur of red. Her throat constricted.

She thought of calling Robin, or maybe Aunt Cassandra, but the phone weighed like lead in her hand. Her head felt too crowded. Instead, she sank onto a stool behind the counter, setting the phone aside and bracing her elbows on her knees. She forced herself to inhale in slow, deliberate pulls of air. The lights above her hummed faintly, and the frigid awareness of what had happened seeped into her bones.

At the same time, in places she could not see, other news outlets were already updating their feeds, fueling the city's appetite for tragic headlines. And somewhere in the city, Ethan was no doubt reading the alerts too. Ivy thought of him without meaning to. Dark hair, that intense gaze, the way he had strolled into her shop and baited her with pointed questions. He had teased about illusions and truth. She had pegged him for a reporter, though she had seen no official press card that day. The entire exchange had felt electric, like he was collecting clues on her. Now, she suspected he would be latching onto this story.

The hours that followed the news alert were a blur of sickening disbelief and churning guilt. Ivy's frantic warning to the police which was met with polite skepticism, had become a preventable tragedy. Just as she feared, Ethan Matson did not just latch onto the story. He ignited a firestorm. His article, published with the brutal efficiency of a seasoned reporter, did not just detail the death at the Powell Street station. It featured the cryptic tale of a local psychic who had tried to warn the authorities hours before the event. By morning, Ivy's name was no longer her own. It had been twisted into a sensational headline. The quiet sanctuary of her shop was shattered by the clamor of the outside world, as the first wave of reporters descended, their cameras and questions hungry for the woman who saw the future.

Ivy pressed her back against the door, heart hammering as she slid the latch shut. Outside, a crush of voices erupted. She felt the vibrations in the glass before she heard them. Reporters calling her name, fingernails tapping on the glass, the click of camera shutters. Her name was everywhere now, taped across local news stations and plastered on social media. *Ivy Lewis, The BART Oracle.* The moniker made her cringe.

She leaned forward and flipped the CLOSED sign. A wave of phone screens lit up outside, and muffled knocks thudded against the window. She had never asked for any of this. She had wanted only to share a warning. Now, a stranger's tragedy clung to her reputation like a stubborn stain. Turning away, she yanked the blinds down to block the curious eyes that peered through the glass. The hollow ring in her ears only worsened as she stepped back into the dim shop.

The Oracle was steeped in the smell of brewed tea and lemon polish, an incongruous comfort set against the chaos outside. She reached for a small lamp, but the overhead fixture cast enough of a glow that it felt too revealing. Let them think she had left. She switched the lamp off again. A haze of late-afternoon shadows settled over the cramped space, crystals glimmering faintly in the half-light. Sliding to the floor, she tucked her knees to her chest. Her phone screen glowed, perched on the edge of the reading table. She had not summoned the courage to look at it since the first notifications poured in. She knew each ping brought fresh speculation about her so-called psychic abilities, about the man who had died, about her visit to the police station. The small device was now a minefield of headlines, like "BART Oracle Predicted Accident: Coincidence or Prophecy?" and "Local Tarot Reader Tied to Shocking Fatality."

Her eyes stung. She wondered how many passersby had recognized her face from the news. Ethan Matson's news story, specifically. That name echoed in her mind every time she squeezed her eyes shut. She recalled the slight tilt to his head as he watched her at the police station, the faint teasing edge in his voice when he had come to the shop. She still could not be certain how he had switched from subtle observer to bold journalist printing her name so widely. Now, there was no ignoring the results. They were arrayed outside, borrowing her life for headlines.

As she expelled a shaky breath, she heard a faint click from outside, followed by the rattle of keys. Anyone else might have panicked, but Ivy recognized the noise. Only one other person had a key to The Oracle. Robin. She inhaled as the door opened slowly. The press undoubtedly saw it, too, and hollered questions at the figure entering.

Robin Tate slid through the crack and shut the door. They locked it again, turned and caught sight of Ivy curled on the floor in the near-darkness. Their eyes went round, but they said nothing right away. Instead, they stepped sideways, parted a corner of the blinds, and peeked outside. When they lowered the blinds, their shoulders slumped.

"You look like you're hiding in a bunker," Robin said softly, crossing to stand over Ivy. "And I guess you are, in a way."

Ivy raised her face. Her voice cracked. "I did lock myself in."

Robin pressed their lips together. "I saw the papers. You're front and center on the local news sites. No wonder the sidewalk is packed." They collapsed onto the small couch against the far wall, dropping a satchel stuffed with old receipts and scheduling lists. "Does this mean no new clients? Or is it ironically good for business?"

A small, humorless laugh escaped Ivy's throat. "I'm not sure. I don't think I want any clients right now." She wiped at her face with the back of her hand. The shame of being singled out, her photograph under a headline like *The BART Oracle*, had shifted from shock to a gnawing ache. "Robin, I never asked for this. I just thought I could stop something terrible from happening."

Robin shook their head. "I know. But apparently, this reporter didn't care about your intentions. He smelled a story. The question is, how did he know in such detail?" They gestured vaguely, referencing the precise quotes in the article. "You either hide," they said, throwing Ivy a pointed look, "or you own it. That's what we have to figure out."

"I can't own it." Ivy's voice wavered. She rose to her feet, feeling an unsteady rush of blood to her head. She moved to the window and peeked out. Reporters still stood there, their cameras pointed at The Oracle's door, waiting for her to reemerge. "Owning it would be normal if it was just a rumor. But this is morbid. A man died, and now people are acting like it's a sideshow."

She turned away again. Her reflection in the glass had shown a pale, haggard face. Dark shadows rimmed her eyes, and her hair was a half-tangled mess from ignoring her morning routine. She snatched her phone and switched it to silent, refusing to let it jolt her with every new alert.

"Well, if you're not going to own it," Robin responded, "you could try ignoring it until it passes. But some reporters will keep digging. I have a bad feeling this BART Oracle thing might last longer than you'd hope."

Ivy stood there, arms folded tight across her chest. She knew stalling would not solve the problem. Should she issue a statement denying her involvement? But that would be a lie. She had gone to the police. And that snippet of truth was enough to fuel every rumor. She also worried that the more she fought back, the more it would look like a publicity stunt.

Robin watched her from the couch. The glow from a salt lamp gave them a slight halo of pinkish light. Their voice turned gentle. "You're not alone in this, okay? We'll figure out a game plan. Just... breathe first. Maybe drink some water."

Ivy's throat felt raw. She nodded and padded toward the small kitchenette. The overhead light in the back came back to life when she flipped the switch. In the quiet, she could almost pretend there was no one outside. She poured water from the sink into a ceramic mug and held it close, letting the cool surface steady her nerves. She sipped the water. Her phone buzzed again, unstoppable, even on silent. The shop lights were off in the front, so the only illumination came from the humming bulb overhead. She lingered there, not wanting to return to the darkened storefront, the big window, and the hungry eyes. She could not stop seeing that man with the red scarf in her nightmares. Now the city wanted to label her with a sensational name that spun it into a spectacle.

Footsteps sounded behind her, and Robin's orange sweater sleeve brushed her elbow. They gave her an encouraging half-smile. "Between the rent and the noise outside, I'd say you probably want to close up for the day. Maybe the next few days." She wanted to thank them, but her voice felt blocked. She took another sip of water, which did not wash away the dread that curdled in her stomach. After a moment, she cleared her throat and whispered, "What if they never stop? What if the city starts calling me a monster? Some people on social media are saying I let a man die to prove I have psychic powers. That I set it up somehow."

Robin's eyes flashed. "That's ridiculous. You tried to warn the police. You did what you thought was right. This is all... twisted. You have to remember that."

Ivy nodded. The tension in her chest loosened, but only slightly. She turned to set her mug in the sink. One day, she thought, this might all blow over. But that did not feel comforting. Her skin prickled with the sense that everything had changed. She was no longer just Ivy, the apathetic tarot reader. She was Ivy, the BART Oracle, whether she wanted it or not.

Robin's phone chimed from inside their pocket. They pulled it out, frowned at the screen, then lowered it. "You have a missed call. Dr. Mercer, from the looks of it." They squinted. "He's left you a voicemail, but I guess someone gave him my number, too?"

Ivy stilled. "Dr. Mercer?" She had not spoken to him in a long time. Once, he had been her therapist, back when the weight of her early nightmares got too heavy for her parents to handle. "Did he say what he needed?"

Robin shook their head. "He just asked for you. Sounds like he wants to help."

Ivy nodded. The notion that Dr. Mercer might actually believe her left her relieved but strangely vulnerable. It reminded her of being much younger, describing menacing shapes from her dreams and expecting an adult to say it was all real. She had never quite gotten that acknowledgment. She felt unsteady as she stepped back into the front of the shop. The phone in her hand glowed with a new ring, this one more insistent. Dr. Mercer's name lit up her caller ID.

She closed her eyes. The reporters were still outside. Robin squeezed her shoulder reassuringly, and slipped away to give her some space. Ivy walked to the corner and answered the call in a whisper.

Dr. Mercer's voice emerged with gentle calm. "Ivy, I'm guessing it's a difficult day. Are you able to talk?"

Her eyes prickled with fresh tears. "It's not a good day," she managed, pressing her palm over her mouth to stifle a sob. "I don't know what's happening. I didn't want all this attention."

"I understand. I read the coverage, although I'm cautious about the slant. I'm not calling as your therapist. I'm calling because you seem genuinely frightened, and that fear deserves to be heard."

Ivy felt her knees weaken. She lowered herself onto the floor behind the round reading table, seeking privacy it provided. She imagined the front window as a stage, with the curtains still drawn back. Out of habit, she touched the deck of tarot cards set beside a dusty quartz crystal. "Everyone thinks I'm a sideshow," she whispered. "But I'm the only one who knows what it felt like, how real it was, that awful dream. I can't make it vanish."

Dr. Mercer remained quiet for a moment. His voice soothed her. "Sometimes, we experience events that defy neat explanations. Whether that is new insight, intense anxiety, or something else, it's not mine to diagnose over the phone. But I believe you when you say you feel unsettled and overwhelmed." He paused gently. "Tell me what you need."

Ivy's chest rose in a trembling breath. "I just want it to stop. The photos, the name, the reporters. I don't want to see my face on the news. And I don't want to be asked if I'm a fraud. I feel like I can't leave my shop."

"I hear that," Dr. Mercer remarked. "Maybe it will help to step away from the public eye. Let your mind breathe. But never think you are alone." A faint echo from his office phone line made a crackle. "You can call me anytime. If you need to meet in person, I'll do what I can."

She realized she was crying softly, shoulders beginning to shake. Emotions were too thick. She felt pinned between wanting to vanish and wanting someone to hold her hand and prove she was not losing her mind.

Dr. Mercer continued, his tone kind. "I don't want to push you if it's too much right now. Just know you can reach out. Sometimes these experiences can jar deeper things awake. It's not unusual to feel changes."

She closed her eyes, pressing the phone to her ear. The weight of his words resonated. Something inside her truly felt changed, as if a thin barrier had cracked. She had tried to warn the police, and it had come true. No matter what the world believed, that event had carved a raw channel in her mind.

She tried to speak but choked on her tears. "I... I think something's wrong with me," she whispered, voice trembling. "Or... maybe something's waking up."

The tears finally spilled freely, and Ivy buried her face in her free hand. Robin hovered in the background, expression concerned, while the reporters' distant calls droned through the covered windows. Nothing felt simple anymore. The quiet was gone, replaced by the drum of her pulse and that creeping sense that her life had cracked open in a way she could not yet fathom.

CHAPTER

FIVE

THE DOUBT

Ivy sat cross-legged on the long, cream-colored sofa in her parents' living room. Faint afternoon light slanted through the gauzy curtains, striping her bare arms with dusty rays. She balanced a photo album on her lap, the edges of its cover frayed. Sticky plastic film no longer pressed smoothly across each page, and a few pictures threatened to slip free.

As she turned a page, her gaze snagged on a photograph of herself as a child, no older than seven, peeking out from behind a half-bent birthday banner. Her hair was pulled into twin pigtails, her expression wide-eyed and earnest. A cluster of neighborhood kids crowded around her, grinning at a bright cake on a table. The memory caught in her throat. Her mother had been in the corner that day, wearing a crisp linen dress and studying Ivy with nervous watchfulness. The camera had captured only a fraction of Anna's expression, but Ivy remembered the tension in her mother's eyes as if it were yesterday. She could practically hear the echo of her mother's clipped whisper. *"You can't just say things like that, Ivy. People will think you're strange."*

Ivy swallowed, running a fingertip along the edge of the photograph. She could still recall the moment vividly. The adults had gathered on the lawn, sipping lemonade and chatting about mundane suburban events, like who had a new car, who was remodeling their kitchen, or who was changing jobs. Ivy had turned to one of the guests, an older family friend, and blurted that his flight home would be canceled. She had not known why she felt so certain, only that an image of an airport monitor flashing *CANCELED* in red had appeared in her mind. Panic had seized her, and she had spoken without thinking.

Laughter had died immediately. Her mother's sharp voice followed. The party had continued, but tension buzzed in the air. The next day, that very man called in awe to report his flight had, in fact, been canceled unexpectedly. No one wanted to acknowledge the strangeness. Instead, everyone seemed eager to forget the incident, except Ivy, who felt more convinced than ever that the flashes in her head pointed toward something real.

She flipped another page. Another photograph of her younger self slid forward, partially unstuck from the page. In this shot, she was perched on a sofa, hugging a bright quilt. Her dark curls framed her face. Mouth half open, she almost seemed like she was mid-prophecy. Ivy stared at the image, feeling an ache in her chest. Her mother's voice floated up from memory, that same scolding.

"You cannot say these things, not if you want to lead a

normal life." Each time Ivy had tried to confide in her mother about the glimpses she saw, Anna shut her down, insisting that the mind created fanciful scenarios, that children craved attention in unusual ways.

Ivy murmured to no one in particular, "Maybe I was strange." It was more than an echo of her mother's words. It was a confession. The house felt oddly still. She glanced around the living room. Stacks of academic journals on neuroscience and psychology lined a nearby bookshelf. The air smelled faintly of lemon polish and the stale dryness of untouched spaces. She had not grown up in a house that fostered imaginative leaps. Logic and proof reigned here.

A quiet rustling preceded the arrival of David Lewis, her father. He stepped in, carrying a small tray with a single teacup. "I thought you might want something to soothe your nerves," he offered, voice gentle.

She glanced up, forcing a small smile. "Thank you, Dad." She carefully lifted the warm cup, pressing it between her palms. He set the tray on a side table, then eased himself onto the sofa beside her. The old cushions dipped under his weight.

David's gaze moved to the open album. "I remember that day," he spoke at last, nodding toward the birthday photograph. "You were so excited about turning seven and being allowed to choose your own decorations."

Ivy tried to laugh, but the sound caught. "I also remember Mom hovering, telling me not to scare the guests."

Her father hesitated. "Your mother... she wanted to

protect you from being labeled or teased." He gave a soft shake of his head. "Neither of us knew how to handle the things you said, the things you saw. We had no frame of reference."

Ivy sipped the tea, welcoming its warmth. Although she had always believed her parents never grasped the weight of her experiences, she had rarely considered that maybe they were simply unprepared.

She kept her gaze on the photograph. "I do know Mom was worried," she whispered softly. "But it felt like rejection."

David leaned forward, elbows plopped on his knees. "Your mother loves you," he replied, voice low. "She fears what she can't define. So do I, sometimes. But that never meant you were broken."

Ivy's cheeks warmed. She recalled the recent tumult. Reporters outside her shop, rumors, the broken trust. The memory of that birthday party melded with what had fallen on her life recently.

Unsure how to respond, she placed the teacup aside and revisited another photograph. In this one, she was older, around nine, standing in front of a science fair display. She looked perfectly normal until one noticed the distant, frowning expression in her eyes, as though she were glimpsing something no child should see. A spark of dread flared in Ivy's chest.

David watched her carefully. "Your mother told me you were... having some difficulties recently. Visions again." He seemed to pick his words with caution. "Is that why you came here?"

"Partly," Ivy admitted, running her thumb over the album cover. She felt a wave of exhaustion. "I needed quiet. I needed a place where I might remember what it felt like not to be, constantly on alert."

He nodded, pressing his lips together. "How can I help?"

She let the silence stretch. She wanted to say she had no idea how he could help, that her life had become too large, too surreal. Yet a flutter of need urged her to accept his presence.

At last, she asked in a small voice, "Do you ever wish I was... normal?"

David blinked in surprise. "Never." When she did not look convinced, he reached out and put a hand on her shoulder. "I might wish life were easier for you. But that doesn't mean you should be less than who you are."

Ivy closed the album and released a shaky breath. She stared at the floral pattern on the sofa cushions, recalling how, in her teenage years, she tried to bury her odd glimpses in diaries, explaining them away as nightmares. In college, she had studied psychology, desperate to label everything as illusions or stress. Nothing erased the moments of absolute clarity. If anything, they grew sharper.

She rubbed a thumb along the edge of the album. "I felt so alone, you know? Especially after that fiasco with the canceled flight. People looked at me like I was the one who caused it. As if I wanted to be singled out."

Her father exhaled, a quiet sigh of regret. "We should

have handled it differently. I keep telling myself we did our best, but I know we could have listened more."

Ivy's heart twisted. She closed her eyes briefly. A faint sound in the hallway signaled her mother's approach. Anna stepped into the living room, hair pinned back, posture upright. She paused at the threshold, eyeing the photo album.

Ivy braced herself. Anna finally came closer. "I thought I heard you two talking," she stated, her tone carefully measured. "Are you... doing all right, Ivy?"

Ivy's throat went dry, but she mustered a nod. "I'm just... remembering," she replied softly.

Anna's gaze drifted to the photographs. "We didn't always handle things well back then," she said, voice beginning to quiver. "But we needed you to fit into a world that doesn't understand these things." Her eyes moved from the album to Ivy. "I wasn't sure how else to keep you safe."

Ivy stood. Conflicting emotions tightened her chest. She wanted to ask why her mother had refused to let her talk, why every extraordinary moment was hidden away as though shameful. Yet seeing the subdued look in Anna's eyes made her hold back. She realized that her mother was, in her own manner, apologizing.

Anna clasped her hands awkwardly. "If you need anything... we're here."

Uncertainty knotted in Ivy's stomach. She wanted solace but was not sure how to accept it from a mother who had always policed her outbursts. Finally, she nodded. Anna lingered another second, then turned, heading back to another part of the house. The air carried a subtle feeling of words unspoken.

Ivy sank to the couch again. David remained beside her, silent but supportive. Outside, a faint gust of wind brushed the windows. A clatter of dishes in the kitchen told her that Anna was likely cleaning or busying herself with chores to relieve her own anxiety.

After a prolonged stillness, Ivy spoke. "Sometimes I think it would be easier if these visions disappeared," she confessed, voice trembling. "I wouldn't have to worry about seeing tragedies before they happen. I wouldn't have to carry the guilt of not stopping them."

David squeezed her shoulder gently. "Or you wouldn't be you," he responded. "You always tried to help others, even as a little girl."

She stared down at the album on her lap, noticing the faded gold lettering that spelled out LEWIS FAMILY PHOTOS. The edges bore coffee stains, a testament to many nights spent reminiscing. Despite the occasional heartbreak, this was still her home, full of complicated care. Her eyes misted. There was a certain comfort in her father's acceptance, even if he could not undo the years of dismissal.

She recalled that old shame from the birthday party that still haunted her dreams. With a trembling hand, she turned one more page. The next photograph showed her parents flanking her at a restaurant booth, arms around her shoulders. She seemed about ten, a little grin hinting at mischief. Perhaps that snapshot was taken on a good day, one when her mother was not so guarded and her father not so anxious. The three of them seemed almost normal.

"I guess... I'm just not sure how to move forward," she admitted quietly. "Maybe I came to see if you'd tell me I was imagining it all, like old times. But I needed to remember who I was before it became... so over-whelming."

David watched her carefully. The lines on his face deepened with sympathy and a trace of regret. "Ivy," he said, "you were never broken. Just... ahead of the rest of us." His words were so gentle and unexpected that she felt her eyes sting with sudden tears.

She gripped his hand, her other arm hugging the photo album close. The clock ticked on, and a fragile warmth blossomed inside her as sunlight shifted across the living room floor. For the first time in a while, she let herself hope that maybe, despite all the cracks in their family and the doubts in her own mind, she could find a way to reconcile the person she had been with the person she was becoming.

SIX

THE RIFT

Ivy sat at the dining table, hands folded stiffly in her lap, while the overhead light cast a yellow sheen on the long wooden surface. A polite clink of silverware broke the silence every few seconds. Her father, David, sat across from her with worry etched into his brow. Anna, her mother, occupied the seat at the head of the table, shoulder blades rigid. Three plates held remnants of grilled vegetables and roasted chicken. No one reached for seconds.

Outside, streetlights glowed through the nighttime fog that pressed against the glass, making the interior silence feel more profound. Ivy sipped water, forcing it past the knot in her throat. She felt Anna's cautious gaze, a spark of scrutiny lurking beneath her calm expression.

"How is your business lately?" Anna asked. Her voice was clipped, devoid of warmth.

Ivy cleared her throat. "It's... all right." All right was a lie. Reporters had posted themselves outside her shop for days. Friends called in frantic bursts, wanting the real story. She had run from that chaos to be here tonight, but here felt no better.

Anna tapped her fork against the plate. "And by business, I mean the... readings. The Oracle shop." She did not look at Ivy. Instead, she stared at the half-eaten food. "I assume all the fuss around you being the BART Oracle has died down."

Her father shifted. "Anna, maybe we should..."

She cut him off. "I want a real answer, David." Her gaze turned to Ivy, cold and direct. "So, has it settled? Or are reporters still putting microphones in your face, demanding an explanation you can't provide?"

Ivy squared her shoulders. "They're still outside," she admitted. "Not as many as before, but enough."

Anna set her fork down with a snap. "You attracted them, Ivy. You gave them a dramatic story, and they ran with it. Are you happy with that? Each day you let them spin some sensational tale about you." She inhaled sharply. "Your father and I are worried."

The nib of anxiety in Ivy's heart flared into something hotter. "Worried that I've told a truth?" she muttered. "Or worried that I'm an embarrassment?"

David reached for her hand across the table, but Ivy kept her arms pinned to her sides.

Anna's knuckles went white around her glass. "This isn't about embarrassment," she contended. "It's about your well-being. The mind can play tricks, especially under stress. You saw something, or thought you did, and convinced yourself it was real. The entire city saw it. That kind of attention... it can be dangerous."

A spike of anger churned in Ivy's chest. She recalled the confusion and fear she had endured. Anna's words sounded eerily from her childhood. She forced her voice level. "You're not curious," she said slowly, "about how I might have known? About how everything I described came true?"

Anna's eyes moved up, meeting Ivy's with a flash of impatience. "I'm more concerned that you think it did." She paused, glancing at her husband. "David, say something."

He hesitated, looking pained. "Ivy," he muttered gently, "we want to keep you safe. You were at our house just a few days ago, looking through old photos... reminding yourself of times when..."

"Times when you both told me I was making things up," Ivy interrupted. The bitterness in her own voice startled her. "All those incidents I tried to explain, times I insisted I saw things before they happened. I was a child, and you never let me speak." She exhaled a shaky breath. "Just once, I want you to say, 'Yes, Ivy, it must have been terrifying. Let's figure it out together.' But you can't, can you?"

Anna closed her eyes for a moment, then pressed the glass to her lips. She took a long, steady sip as though she was gathering resolve. When she set the glass down, her gaze hardened. "I'm scared that you think you knew," she said. "Truly knew. That certainty is dangerous. It keeps you from questioning. If you'd come to me and admitted you needed help, we could have found a doctor, or a specialist, or…"

"That again," Ivy spat under her breath. "This isn't a delusion, Mom. Someone died, exactly the way I saw."

"Ivy, please," David pleaded, but she could barely hear him. Blood roared in her ears.

"Remember that party years ago," Ivy continued, voice rising, "where I warned that man his flight would be canceled? Everyone stared at me like I was a freak. The next day, it happened. You still said it was a coincidence. That dismissal never stopped."

Anna's nostrils flared. "Because if I had encouraged you, you might have grown up thinking every dream was a prophecy. It is not healthy. This city is dotted with enough charlatans who call themselves psychic. I couldn't let my only daughter become another sideshow."

A tremor moved through Ivy's hands. She realized she was shaking, all the resentment she had buried now bubbling to the surface. "You didn't protect me," she retorted, her anger and hurt carried on each syllable. "You erased me." The words felt raw, but she knew they were true. Tears blurred the edges of her vision, but she refused to let them fall.

David stood, stepping around his chair, but Ivy flinched away. "Don't," she muttered. Her father froze. Outside, a bus rumbled down the street, its headlights sweeping across the drawn curtains.

Anna stared at Ivy, color rising in her cheeks. Her jaw was clenched. "I never erased you. I tried to save you from an abnormal path. I believed you had a choice to be normal. You act like that's some kind of betrayal."

Ivy let loose a broken laugh, bitterness coating each breath. "It is a betrayal. You didn't stand by me when I needed you most. You wanted to shape me into your definition of normal." Her pulse thundered. She shoved her chair back, rattling the table. She grabbed her coat from the back of the chair and thrust her arms into the sleeves. "I'm done," she snapped, glaring at her mother. "I'm done asking for permission to be what I am."

David held up his hands in a plea. "Ivy, let's talk this through."

She shook her head. "I can't do this. I came here hoping... for something else. This was a mistake." She threw one last glance at her mother, whose face had gone strangely ashen.

Anna said nothing, eyes fixed on the patterns of the tablecloth. Ivy's heart hammered. She turned on her heel and strode toward the door. Her head was filled with words she wanted to hurl at them, accusations about all the times they stifled her questions, but breath was short in her lungs. She pushed out into the night, leaving the thick quiet of the house behind. The cold air slapped her cheeks. Fog curled through the streetlamps like winding ghosts, and she pressed her coat collar closer around her neck as she marched down the driveway. She half expected her father to follow, but no footsteps sounded behind her.

Unspent emotion raged inside her. She had no clue where she was heading. She only knew she needed space, away from her parents' living room. Blocks passed in a blur. She turned a corner into a better-lit street, catching her breath. Eventually, she realized she was in Nob Hill, a district known for its old architecture and steep sidewalks. A memory stirred of the townhouse covered in creeping ivy vines, a place where her aunt Cassandra lived. She slowed in front of the townhouse steps. The porch lights glowed faintly, revealing a door with detailed brass fixtures. Cassandra's place stood like a guardian in the haze.

Ivy paused, arms hugging her middle. She had visited her aunt only once since the fiasco at the Oracle gained traction. Cassandra had been cryptic, offering half-answers about family history. Ivy's parents never wanted her to spend time here for fear of "encouraging illusions," but right now, she did not care. Maybe Cassandra was the only person bold enough to tell her something real.

She climbed the steps and rapped her knuckles on the door. Her heart thumped, half-regretting this decision. After a few moments, the lock turned with a faint click. The door opened partway, revealing Cassandra Vale's poised silhouette. Candlelight from within outlined the side of her face, accentuating her sharp features. She wore a dark, flowing cardigan that draped over one shoulder.

"Ivy," Cassandra exclaimed. Her voice was low, carrying a note of concern. "Something tells me you've had quite a night."

Ivy swallowed, blinking back the heat in her eyes. "Dinner with my parents," she said flatly. "It turned into a complete...meltdown."

Cassandra's gaze shifted behind Ivy as if checking for watchers. Then she addressed Ivy in a gentle tone. "Come inside. You look cold."

Ivy stepped over the threshold, her shoulders still tense. The interior smelled of sandalwood incense and old pages, a welcome shift from the damp chill outside. Cassandra guided her into a narrow foyer, richly decorated with warm-colored rugs and intricate tapestries. The house felt timeless.

When the door clicked shut, Ivy issued a shaky breath. "I'm sorry to show up like this," she said. "I just... I don't know where else to go. My mother still thinks I'm imagining everything." She lifted her gaze to meet Cassandra's. "I want the truth, whatever it is. I want to know why these visions keep getting stronger. Why none of this feels like a coincidence."

A glint of emotion crossed Cassandra's face. She motioned for Ivy to follow her down a dim corridor. At the end, they entered a small sitting room lit by a single lamp. A bookshelf stood against one wall, crowded with old volumes. On a small table, a half-burned candle quivered. The only sound was the soft whir of the heater.

Cassandra gestured for Ivy to sit on a cushioned chair. Ivy sank into it, hugging her coat around her. Her aunt settled on a nearby chaise, the lamplight catching the silver strands in her hair. Ivy's voice trembled as she repeated, "Tell me the truth. All of it." She felt hollow and desperate. "I've had enough of half-answers. I need to know why I'm dreaming of things that come true. I need to know why it feels like I'm on the edge of something big."

For a long moment, Cassandra studied her, lips pressed tight. The hush stretched as though the house itself waited for her answer. "You're convinced you want everything," Cassandra offered softly. Lines of tension framed her eyes. "But you may not be ready for it."

Ivy forced her shoulders straight. "I'm tired of being treated like a child. Whatever the cost, I can handle it." She set her jaw. "Please. I want the full story about us. Our family. My... gift."

Cassandra exhaled. She pressed one hand against a stack of worn journals on an end table. "You're not ready," she maintained, her voice quiet. She added, "But I suppose the truth doesn't care."

CHAPTER

SEVEN

THE PATTERN

Everything about the townhouse felt slightly off. The place was unchanged from her last visit, yet something felt different, like the shadows in the corners had deepened, waiting for a secret to be revealed. The walls were lined floor to ceiling with shelves of mismatched books. Every surface illuminated by candle flames. Instead of a coffee table, a large trunk draped in a woven blanket stood at the center of the room. Cassandra halted before it, her silver-streaked hair gathered at the back of her neck with an ornate clasp. She felt as if she had stepped into a cloister cut off from time, a space that had no place for the frantic pace or clamor that dominated her life elsewhere in San Francisco.

Cassandra crouched and traced the trunk's latch with steady fingers, then flipped it open. From inside, she lifted four leather-bound journals. Their covers bore small scuffs, but gold leaf patterns still caught the lamplight. Twisting vines, crescent moons, and strange runes.

"These were your grandmother's," Cassandra murmured, placing the journals on the trunk. "And mine."

Ivy approached, breath catching. She had heard small rumors as a child about her grandmother's visions, but Anna had always dismissed those stories as folklore. Yet here lay tangible proof of a legacy no one had explained. Cassandra opened the top journal. Its spine cracked softly. The pages, sepia-toned and fragile, were filled with ink lines forming strange symbols. Some pages held rough sketches of faces or objects, while others contained neat rows of sentences in a language Ivy did not recognize. The scent of old paper and faint incense drifted upward. Ivy's pulse thudded in her ears.

"Your grandmother first experienced visions when she was a girl," Cassandra said, eyes on the journal. "Not unlike you. She grew up trying to puzzle out the messages. These entries show her early attempts to record everything she saw."

Ivy's chest tightened. "So, I'm not the first to... see those flashes."

"Not the first," Cassandra agreed. "Not the last. But it's more than seeing." She turned a few pages. "When I was young, I copied her method because I believed it might help me control my own glimpses. We called this our 'family library.' But your mother wanted no part of it."

Ivy's gaze travelled to the bookshelves lining the walls. "I wish someone had shown me these before," she murmured, a note of hurt in her voice.

Cassandra paused on a page featuring a rough sketch of a man wearing a red scarf. The lines were shaky but clear enough to show a figure caught mid-step. Beneath the drawing, a name was scratched out so thoroughly that only the first letter remained. L.

Ivy's pulse sped up. Though the face in the sketch lacked detail, the scarf was identical to one she had seen in her vision of the BART accident. "That's him," Ivy whispered, leaning closer. "I saw a man just like that, moments before he..." She trailed off, remembering the unstoppable dread that had accompanied the vision. Her breath stuttered at the memory.

Cassandra lifted her chin. "These dreams," she said, tapping the page, "they match a pattern your grandmother chronicled. She believed certain images, like the red scarf, were more than random warnings. They were pieces of a larger tapestry, triggers that set events in motion."

The tingle in Ivy's fingers intensified as she ran her hand over the page. She felt the faint ridges where a pen had pressed into paper decades ago. "Then they're not meaningless," she said. "It's like they connect."

"They do," Cassandra confirmed. "They ripple outward. One vision snags a thread of another, each building on the last. Sometimes they converge and become real. Sometimes they warn us of what could be." She closed the journal and placed her palm on the worn cover. "Your grandmother used to say that a vision was never an ending, only a beginning of new possibilities."

Ivy remembered the fear in her mother's voice. If Anna had allowed her to see these journals, maybe she would have felt less alone. "So, I'm not crazy," she echoed.

Cassandra's expression softened. "No," she said. "This is always how it starts." Something in Cassandra's tone implied both caution and acceptance. Ivy sank onto a nearby ottoman, mindful not to disturb the dusty volumes scattered around her. A wave of relief coursed through her, but it arrived hand in hand with dread. If she was truly a part of this legacy, her visions were about more than random flashes. They could shape events she barely understood.

She lifted her gaze to Cassandra. "Why do you have these now? Did you keep them hidden all this time?"

Her aunt closed the trunk gently. "I did. I was afraid. Too many mistakes were made." She paused, pressing her lips together. "And I wasn't sure you were ready."

Heat pricked behind Ivy's eyes. "I've been desperate for an explanation since I was a child," she said, her voice quivering. "I spent years believing I was either delusional or cursed. But you…"

"I thought I was protecting you," Cassandra interrupted, her tone subdued. "Your mother believed that burying this knowledge would let you grow up normal. I… let her believe that was best. I left because I felt I couldn't stand by and watch you be stifled. Yet I was also too afraid to challenge her." Her shoulders slumped. "I had my own reasons."

Ivy fell silent, grappling with a swell of bitterness. "If it's in me, I deserve to know how to handle it," Ivy said. "Don't you think?"

Cassandra nodded. "I do. Which is why we're here." She carefully opened the second journal. The handwriting inside was smaller, more deliberate. Ivy leaned in, noticing an intricate chart. Arrows connected symbols. Eyes, flames, crescents, lines crossing in star-like patterns. She recognized faint echoes of her own scribbles. "These," Cassandra said, pointing at the clusters of symbols, "were our attempts to map how one dream led to another. Your grandmother believed that we each tap into a larger web. When one part vibrates, we feel echoes in our own reality."

Ivy traced a finger over the chart. "A web," she murmured. "So, if I see something, like the red scarf, someone else in our family might have seen it too? Or we set something in motion?"

Cassandra sighed. "Possibly both. The tricky part is understanding that once you glimpse a future, you may start guiding it, consciously or not."

Ivy shivered. The memory of the BART tragedy flashed through her mind, conjuring the screech of metal against rails. Had her vision set it in motion, or had she only glimpsed what was inevitable?

Cassandra's gaze moved to the windows, where the ivy outside stretched across the glass panes. "I don't say any of this lightly," she said. "The knowledge in these journals carries danger. It can lure you into thinking you should intervene or withdraw. Either action has consequences."

The gleam of a candle drew Ivy's attention to a small mirror on the far side of the room. It caught her reflection. She saw her own wide eyes, the uncertain tilt of her mouth. For a moment, she wished Ethan were there, though she was not sure how he would handle this conversation. Yet there had been times recently when his unwavering gaze offered steadiness. A pang tightened her chest. She had chosen to come here alone, needing answers from her aunt that no one else could provide.

She turned back to Cassandra. "I want to understand," she said, voice quieter now. "Everything."

"Let me show you." Cassandra motioned for Ivy to bring her an armful of journals. One by one, they spread them out on the trunk. The air smelled of old parchment and faint sandalwood. Ivy brushed her fingertips over the covers, reading the spidery handwriting. Notations of dates, cryptic references, like "R.S. repeats thrice" or "Bridge crossing reversed." Some lines were crossed out or heavily inked over. Others carried short question marks, as if the writer had never deciphered the puzzle.

"Your grandmother called them sequences," Cassandra explained. "A single symbol might reappear in different contexts, leading to multiple branching visions. The question is which path becomes real in the end."

Ivy felt her heart pound. "And the scratched out names?"

Cassandra turned to one especially marked page. "Some references were too dangerous to keep visible," she said. "We believed hiding them might unravel certain outcomes."

Ivy exhaled slowly, absorbing the weight of these revelations. She recalled nights in her shop, doodling images that haunted her. Until now, she had never imagined a complex system linking them. "What if I make a mistake interpreting them?" she asked, voice trembling.

Cassandra closed the journal. "You do your best to correct it," she replied. "But be gentle with yourself. This gift doesn't come with a manual. Your grandmother wrote everything she could, and I added my experiences, but we're both flawed record keepers, shaped by fear and hope."

The confession settled on Ivy's shoulders like a weighted cloak. She realized how human and fragile her grandmother must have been, scribbling furiously to make sense of these wonders and terrors. And how Cassandra, for all her poise and knowledge, also carried scars. She wondered if that was why her aunt's voice held faint sorrow whenever she spoke of the past.

A soft knock on the doorframe startled them. A quiet neighbor who sometimes delivered produce held a small bag brimming with fresh herbs.

"Leave it on the table, please," Cassandra said gently. The man set it down and retreated.

Cassandra waited until the footsteps receded. Then she pulled out a small, leather pouch from her sweater pocket and handed it to Ivy. Inside, Ivy saw a set of thin, rectangular cards, a homemade deck, edges worn from use. The illustrations were faint pencil drawings of weather patterns, clouds, or jagged lightning. "Before your grandmother married," Cassandra continued, "she used these cards to prompt her visions, letting them guide her. If you'd like, you can use them as a starting point. They might help you focus."

Ivy turned over the top card, featuring a simple design of waves curling around a moon. She felt a tingle, not unlike the one she experienced when touching her own tarot deck. "Thank you," she said softly. "I want to try."

Cassandra nodded. "No matter what you see, remember you have a choice," she said. "You can record it, share it, act on it, or ignore it. But it's your path to walk."

Ivy swallowed the lump in her throat. For so long, she had felt powerless. Now, for the first time, she sensed there might be purpose in her visions. The idea both comforted and unnerved her. "Is it normal to feel... split?" she asked. "Half of me wants to run from these journals, and the other half wants to devour every page."

A fleeting smile broke Cassandra's solemnity. "Completely normal." She gestured at the journals. "Take them slowly. Or all at once." Her smile faded. "Just know there is a cost to seeing more."

Silence settled as Ivy wondered what that cost might be. She glanced down at the drawing of the red-scarfed man, her mind going back to that day at the police station, the officer's doubtful gaze, and the confusion that landed her in the public eye as *The BART Oracle*. She felt the ripple of Cassandra's words in her chest. The sequences. The triggers. She ran a trembling hand along the spine of the top journal again. There, etched in faint ink, she made out part of her grandmother's initials. *M. L.* "I wish I'd met her," Ivy whispered.

"She had her faults," Cassandra said. "But she was unstoppable when she believed in something."

Ivy stared at the vines on the cover, imagining a fierce,

determined woman fighting to interpret the swirling chaos of her own mind. It gave Ivy hope. She closed the journal carefully, as though it might crumble under the wrong touch. "Thanks for showing me this," she said. "It means more than you know.

Cassandra inclined her head. "I should have done it sooner." She drew in a breath. "Will you stay here tonight? Or do you have somewhere else you need to be?

Ivy hesitated, thinking of the texts possibly waiting on her phone. She thought of Ethan, of Robin, of her parents. But the urge to remain in this timeless cocoon pulled at her. She wanted to dive into every page, searching for a reflection of her own dreams.

"I'll stay," she said at last, her voice quiet but resolute. Part of her still trembled, uncertain whether she was ready for what she might discover in these journals. Another part was fiercely eager, ready to open the door onto a future she had only glimpsed in broken pieces.

Cassandra rested a hand on Ivy's shoulder. The contact felt warm, anchoring. "You're not crazy," she repeated, voice gentle yet charged with emphasis. "You are simply cracked open. That crack lets the light in."

The final syllables lingered in the room. Ivy exhaled, absorbing the words, letting them settle in her bones. She curled her fingers around the homemade deck her aunt had given her. Dust motes still floated in that amber glow, and the townhouse remained absolute. Ivy gazed at the journals, at Cassandra's steady presence, and at her own reflection in the mirror. She felt something fragile stir in her chest, an acceptance of who she might be.

She closed her eyes for just a moment. A quiet promise formed in her mind. She would listen to these new truths, follow them wherever they led. For the first time in a long while, the sense of impending doom did not suffocate her. Instead, it invited her to discover the pattern hidden in the chaos, and to trust that the shape those ripples formed might be her own.

EIGHT

THE WEIGHT OF INK

The Oracle was a fortress against the encroaching San Francisco night. Ivy had flipped the sign to CLOSED hours ago, drawing the heavy velvet blinds and locking the door not just against potential customers, but against the entire churning, indifferent city. Inside, a sacred quiet had fallen, punctuated only by the soft hiss of a burning sage stick and the gentle rustle of ancient paper. The air was a familiar cocktail of lavender and sandalwood.

She and Robin were huddled in the back room, the small space usually reserved for storing inventory and brewing tea transformed into a makeshift historical archive. The leather-bound journals Cassandra had entrusted her with were spread across the small wooden table, their worn covers looking like sleeping creatures in the warm, glinting candlelight. A half-empty pot of chamomile tea sat between them, its steam long since vanished.

Ivy's heart beat with a strange, syncopated rhythm, one part terror, two parts exhilaration. For the first time, she was not just stumbling through the dark. She had a map, however cryptic and terrifying. She had a history.

"So, she just... handed them over?" Robin asked, their voice a low murmur. They leaned forward, their hair catching the light like a fragmented rainbow. Their usual punk-witchy vibe was softened by an expression of intense focus, their multiple piercings glinting as they stared at the journals with a reverence that matched Ivy's own. "After all these years of ghosting you, Aunt Cassandra decides tonight's the night for a family legacy info-dump?"

Ivy shrugged, running a trembling finger over the gilded, twisting vines on the cover of the top journal.

"So let's see what skeletons your grandma was hiding in these literary closets."

With a deep breath, Ivy opened the first journal. The spine let out a soft, protesting crackle. The pages were filled with the elegant script of a woman she had never met. The ink had faded from black to a soft sepia, and the pages were filled with not just words, but sketches that were frantic, beautiful, and haunting.

They started slowly, a sense of archaeological reverence keeping their movements careful. Ivy would read a fragmented entry aloud, her voice barely a whisper, and Robin would lean in, their intuition a tangible presence in the small room.

"The birds came again today," Ivy read from an entry dated nearly sixty years ago. *"They spelled a word against*

the bruised twilight, but it dissolved before I could grasp it. The message is close, I feel it. A ringing in my bones. But the air is heavy with static."

Beside the entry was a delicate sketch of a murmuration of starlings, their collective shape almost, but not quite, forming a legible word.

"That's one of yours," Robin said instantly. "You told me about the sky-writing birds. You said they felt like a warning you couldn't decipher."

"She saw them, too," Ivy breathed, a chill tracing its way up her spine. It was one thing for Cassandra to tell her she was part of a lineage. It was another to see the proof in ink, to feel the echo of her own visions across the gulf of decades. She felt a profound, aching connection to this woman, this grandmother who had wrestled with the same invisible currents.

They kept reading, falling into a rhythm. Ivy was the vessel, the one who could feel the faint psychic residue left on the pages, and Robin, the interpreter, the one who could see the poetry in the chaos.

They found more recurring symbols, the ones Cassandra had hinted at. The red scarf, sketched hastily on a page corner, with the note, *"A thread of fate. When pulled, all unravels."* There was the bridge, sometimes whole and arching toward a sunlit shore, other times depicted as a skeletal ruin plunging into black water. *"The crossing is a choice,"* she had written. *"To step onto the bridge is to accept the destination, seen or unseen."*

"She's not just recording visions," Robin mused, tapping a finger against a drawing of a single, perfect crescent moon. "She's trying to build a belief system around them. A mythology. To give the chaos meaning."

"Or to control it," Ivy countered, her voice tight. She flipped to a page that made her stomach clench. It was a frantic charcoal sketch of a room on fire, flames licking at the walls, a figure trapped behind a window. It was so eerily similar to the vision she had of Ethan that she felt the phantom heat on her skin again. Beside it, Mireya had written in a shaky hand, *"The fire cleanses, but it also consumes. I fear I have fed it too much of myself."*

"Ivy?" Robin's voice was soft, pulling her back from the edge of the memory. "You okay? You look like you just saw a ghost."

"I think I did," Ivy whispered. She did not elaborate, not yet ready to speak of her premonition of Ethan. It felt too raw, too personal. Instead, she pointed to another recurring image, one that appeared again and again, in both her grandmother's and Cassandra's journals. A shattered mirror.

The drawings were always slightly different. Sometimes it was a handheld looking glass, cracked down the middle. Other times, it was a full-length mirror, exploded into a thousand glittering shards, with a wide, terrified eye reflected in each piece.

But Robin saw something else. *"Fractured self. Seeing yourself in pieces, not knowing which reflection is the real you. It is the fear of losing your identity to the visions."* Their eyes met Ivy's, full of a deep, knowing empathy. "It's what you've been feeling all along, isn't it?"

Ivy could only nod, a lump forming in her throat.

Robin had an uncanny ability to slice through the noise and name the core of her fear. That was their gift, as real and as potent as her own.

As the hours bled into one another, the initial exhilaration began to fade, replaced by a creeping dread. The journals were not just a legacy. They were a warning. They found entries detailing agonizing migraines, periods of deep depression, and a terrifying sense of isolation. Mireya wrote of locking herself away for days, afraid that her visions might bleed into reality and harm her family. Cassandra's entries were more clinical, but no less frightening. She documented experiments, attempts to "trigger" or "contain" specific visions, often with disastrous results. One entry simply read, *"The illusion bit back today. The scars will be a reminder to never again ask for a truth I am not prepared to receive."*

Then, in Cassandra's journal, they found it. A new section, the pages less worn, the ink a starker black. It began with a meticulous drawing of a circular symbol, an eye whose iris was an intricate labyrinth. Radiating from it were seven smaller symbols.

"We've seen this before," Ivy said, pointing to the smaller icons. "The flame, the wave… but these other ones are new." She leaned closer, her breath catching. "And look at this." She indicated a series of names listed beside the main symbol, most of them crossed out with a thick, final stroke of ink. Only one name remained legible.

Lucien.

The name meant nothing to her, but it seemed to vibrate on the page, charged with a dark, malevolent energy. A fleeting image flashed behind Ivy's eyes. A man with hair the color of platinum, his eyes pale and elegant, a cruel smile playing on his lips. She gasped, stumbling back from the table, her chair scraping loudly against the floor.

"Ivy!" Robin was on their feet in an instant, their hands on her shoulders, steadying her. "Breathe. Just breathe. What did you see?"

"A man," Ivy choked out, her heart hammering against her ribs. "He... I think his name is Lucien. He was smiling, but it wasn't kind. It was... hungry." She shuddered, the image already fading, leaving behind only an icy residue of fear.

"Okay," Robin said, their voice a firm, grounding anchor of Ivy's mind. "Okay, that's enough of that journal for tonight." They reached over and gently closed the book, as if shutting a door on a dangerous entity. "Whoever this Lucien guy is, he's bad news. We'll deal with him later. Right now, you need to ground yourself."

They guided her to one of the plush chairs in the main shop area, pushing a cup of lukewarm tea into her hands. "Drink," they commanded. "And tell me something real. What did you have for lunch?"

The question was so mundane, so jarringly normal, that it worked. Ivy blinked, focusing on Robin's concerned face. "A... a turkey sandwich," she managed, the words feeling clumsy in her mouth.

"Good," Robin said with a nod. "Was it on sourdough? I hope it was on sourdough."

A small, watery laugh escaped Ivy's lips. "It was."

"See? The world hasn't ended. Turkey sandwiches still exist." They smiled, a genuine, warm expression that slowly began to chase the chill from Ivy's bones.

It was in that moment of fragile calm that the bell above the shop door chimed.

The sound was so unexpected, so intrusive, that they both froze. Ivy's head snapped toward the front of the shop, her heart leaping into her throat. They were closed. Locked. No one should be here.

Robin moved instantly, their body a protective shield between Ivy and the door. "Stay here," they whispered, their eyes narrowed.

Heavy footsteps approached the curtain that separated the back room from the shop. A silhouette appeared against the thin fabric, tall and broad-shouldered. The curtain was pushed aside, and Ethan Matson stepped into the room.

The atmosphere shifted instantly, the cozy, candlelit intimacy shattering into a thousand pieces of tense, awkward silence. Ethan looked tired, his journalist-handsome features etched with lines of conflict. He had a folded newspaper tucked under his arm, and his intense blue-gray eyes darted from the scattered journals to Ivy's pale face.

"I knocked, but..." he started, his voice trailing off as he took in the scene. He looked from Ivy's wide, fearful eyes to Robin's hostile stance. "I'm sorry. Is this a bad time?"

"It's a *closed* time," Robin shot back, their tone like chipped ice. "As in, not open. As in, go away."

Ethan's gaze shifted to Ivy, a silent appeal in his eyes. "I needed to talk to you, Ivy. It's important."

Ivy found her voice, though it felt thin and reedy. "I don't think we have anything to talk about, Ethan." The hurt from his article, the sting of being turned into a public spectacle as 'The BART Oracle,' was still a fresh wound. She had seen the headlines, the way he had taken her terror and spun it into a sensational story. He had used her.

He took a step forward, his hands raised in a placating gesture. "Please. Just five minutes. I... I need to apologize."

"An apology?" Robin scoffed, taking another step forward to block his path. "You plastered her face all over the news, turned her life into a circus, and now you want to apologize? A little late for that, don't you think?"

"I know," Ethan said, his voice low and earnest. He was looking only at Ivy now. "I know I messed up. I was following a story, doing my job, and I didn't think about the person. I didn't think about you. And I was wrong. Terribly wrong."

Ivy wrapped her arms around herself, a fragile shield. "You didn't just not think, Ethan. You actively chose not to. You saw me at the police station, you heard how distressed I was, and you still ran the story. You saw a headline, not a human being."

The words hit their mark. He flinched, a shadow of guilt crossing his face. "You're right," he admitted, his voice barely a whisper. "I saw an angle, a mystery, and I pursued it. It's what I'm good at. But I can't... I can't ignore what happened. The BART accident... it was real. Exactly like you said. And I can't reconcile that with the world I thought I lived in."

He ran a hand through his perpetually messy hair, a gesture of profound frustration. "I don't know what's happening. I don't understand any of it. But I know that I hurt you, and it's the one fact in this whole insane mess that I can't spin or explain away. I'm sorry."

The sincerity in his voice was a tangible thing, a weight in the quiet room. Ivy's anger, which had been a hot, protective flame, began to waver, leaving behind only the cold ache of betrayal. She hated the part of her that wanted to believe him, the part that was still drawn to his intensity, to the trace of vulnerability she saw in his eyes.

He noticed the journals then, his reporter's curiosity a reflex he could not suppress. His eyes widened slightly. "What are these?"

"None of your business," Robin snapped.

But Ivy just shook her head, a bitter smile touching her lips. "It's my family history," she said, her voice flat. "Apparently, I come from a long line of 'curiosities' you'd love to write about."

The jab landed harder than a physical blow. Ethan looked down at the floor, his shoulders slumping. "That's not why I'm here," he said quietly. "I'm not looking for a story anymore." He looked up, his gaze holding hers, and the raw confusion in his eyes was so potent it made her own heart ache. "I think I'm looking for the truth. And I think, for the first time in my life, I'm terrified of what I might find."

The confession hung in the air between them, fragile and dangerous. He was admitting his fear, his doubt, his crumbling worldview. He was offering her a piece of his broken-and-healing self, and she did not know what to do with it.

She wanted to scream at him, to tell him to leave and never come back. She wanted to throw the journals at him and demand he make sense of them, since he was the one who craved facts and evidence. Most of all, and most terrifyingly, she wanted to step forward and tell him that she was scared, too.

But she did none of those things. The trust between them was a shattered mirror, and she was not sure if it could ever be pieced back together.

"I think you should go," she said finally, her voice so quiet it was almost swallowed by the glittering candlelight.

He looked like he wanted to argue, to plead his case further, but he saw the finality in her expression. He gave a slow, defeated nod. "Okay," he said. He placed the folded newspaper he had been carrying on the edge of a nearby shelf. "I brought you this. It's... it's a copy of a different paper. One that ran a follow-up, a more compassionate piece. It talks about the victim, his family. It makes him human. I thought... I thought you should have it."

He turned and walked out of the room without another word. The curtain swished back into place, and a moment later, the bell on the front door chimed its lonely farewell.

Ivy and Robin stood in silence, the space where he had been feeling both empty and charged. Ivy stared at the curtain, her heart a tangled knot of anger, pity, and a longing she refused to name.

Robin let out a long, slow breath. "Well," they said, their voice losing its hard edge. "That was… a lot."

Ivy did not respond. She walked over to the shelf and picked up the newspaper Ethan had left. She unfolded it, her eyes scanning the article. He was right. It was not about her. It was about the man who had died, a life cut short. It was a piece written with empathy, with respect. It was an apology in newsprint.

She folded it carefully and placed it on the table, next to the journals filled with the secrets of her past. She was surrounded by ink and history, by the weight of things seen and things unsaid. Ethan's apology had not fixed anything, not really. But it had changed something. He had not just seen her as a headline. Maybe, he was starting to learn.

She looked at Robin, who was watching her with gentle, worried eyes.

"You think he meant it?" Robin asked softly.

"I don't know," Ivy whispered, tracing the labyrinth symbol in Cassandra's journal with a shaking finger.

NINE

THE COLLAPSE

Ivy perched behind a small folding table draped in purple fabric, surveying the teeming energy of the metaphysical fair. Soft string lights glowed overhead, transforming the cavernous expo hall into a patchwork of intimacy. Heavy incense perfumed the air. Nearby, she heard the steady pulse of a hand drum as a group of vendors chanted and danced in a pointed circle. The echo of each beat vibrated in her own heartbeat.

It had been a full week since the initial uproar around her had quieted. Reporters used to line up outside her shop, but most had turned to a new headline. Only a few stragglers still lurked online, posting speculative threads on social media about her so-called gift. She had stopped checking. It was easier to pretend her life was settling.

She inhaled slowly. The fair was organized by a local metaphysical society. They offered crystals, aura readings, small group meditations, and booths for every holistic craft. Ivy normally liked these gatherings. She would set up a table, accept the modest reading fee, and give gentle, uplifting guidance to curious visitors. Today her heart fluttered with uneasy tension. She was going through the motions, flipping her tarot cards or smiling at passersby, but she felt strangely disconnected.

Her friend, Robin Tate, was stationed a few tables away. They had insisted on accompanying her. Brightly colored scarves framed Robin's short, vibrant hair, and they caught Ivy's eye, wiggling their fingers in an encouraging wave. She returned a tight-lipped smile.

A tall candle flared at the corner of Ivy's table. She offered brief introductions and asked if they wanted one-card pulls or deeper readings. Most wore polite, curious expressions, likely drawn by the rumor of her "uncanny predictions." Yet her cards felt heavy. She repeated the same standard lines, cautioning that tarot was a tool for personal insight, not a definitive prophecy. The sincerity in her voice wavered.

A silver-haired woman with bright amber jewelry approached, then drifted away when Ivy's posture slumped. Another person hovered indecisively and chose a different reader across the aisle. Ivy exhaled a shaky breath and rubbed her temples. A headache was edging in. She centered herself by focusing on the melodic drumming that drifted across the rows of booths. One of the organizers had told her this event was meant to be an energetic reset for the community. She had almost laughed. Her aunt's words from a week ago, about old journals, family lineages, the visions, still circled in her thoughts. *"You're cracked open,"* Cassandra had said, an ominous statement that rang in Ivy's ears each time she tried to sleep.

She saw movement out of the corner of her eye. A woman in a flowing blue shawl whose edges glimmered with gold-thread embroidery paused at Ivy's table. Her hair was dark and pinned in a low bun, and her brown eyes held a mix of caution and curiosity. She hesitated, glancing over the array of crystals and the little sign that read, "Psychic Insight with Ivy Lewis." Then she stepped forward.

"Hello," Ivy said softly, gesturing toward the folding chair opposite her.

The woman sat, drawing the shawl around her shoulders. Incense cast gentle patterns of drifting smoke between them. "I'm Mariella," she said. Her voice trembled slightly. "I saw... some posts online mentioning you. That maybe you had a real gift."

Ivy cleared her throat. She forced the corners of her mouth upward. "I'll do my best," she murmured. "You can shuffle these cards, if you like."

She pushed a deck forward. Mariella picked them up, riffling once or twice. Her eyes fluttered shut as if making a silent wish. She handed the deck back. Ivy spread the cards in a simple fan. A muscle in her neck tensed.

"Choose three," Ivy said.

Mariella drew the cards and placed them, face-down, on the purple cloth. Ivy flipped them in a slow, deliberate rhythm. She wanted to focus on the images, but a fuzzy pressure crept behind her eyes. She saw the Ten of Swords in reverse. She saw the Moon. She saw the Knight of Cups inverted.

"Are you... do you see anything unusual?" Mariella asked.

Ivy blinked. "The Ten of Swords reversed can sometimes mean rising from a low point," she explained, voice measured. "The Moon suggests hidden truths or illusions. And the Knight of Cups reversed... maybe emotional turbulence." She forced a gentle smile, fighting the slight flutter in her lungs. "All of these can remind you to..."

She broke off. An unexpected wave of heat flared across her forehead. She swallowed hard. Sweat prickled at the back of her neck. Mariella's face became fuzzy at the edges. Ivy pressed the heel of her hand against her brow, dazed. She tried to form a reassuring statement, but the words refused to organize. "Apologies, I might need a sip of water."

Before she could reach for the bottle, the woman grasped her free hand. "Are you all right?"

The contact sent a jolt through Ivy's skin. A door swung open inside her mind. A flood of images rushed at her. The drumming receded, replaced by something else. She saw the outline of a rusted metal bridge, water churning below, the roar of wind howling around iron beams. A girl clung to the rails, her cries lost to the rush of a furious current. The image shattered, bathed in stark, white noise, accompanied by an agonized scream. Ivy's breath caught.

Reality lurched back around her with a painful snap. She realized she had wrenched her hand free. Her chest rose and fell in panicked bursts. Mariella stared at her, eyes wide with alarm.

"What did you see?" Mariella whispered.

Ivy tried to steady her voice, but her ears buzzed with an echo of that scream. She clutched the corner of her table, knocking an amethyst crystal to the floor. "I... it was..." Her own thoughts refused to line up. She just knew that some violent future had flashed through her mind.

The overhead lights swam. She heard quick footsteps from behind her. Robin's voice was calling her name, but it sounded distant. *Keep it together*, Ivy told herself. She could not recall if she had eaten breakfast today. She felt hot and cold, all at once. The wave of dizziness slammed into her with the force of a physical blow. She accidentally shoved the table, causing the tarot cards to scatter onto the carpet. A half-burned candle slid and fell. Mariella reached for Ivy, but Ivy stumbled backward. Pressure built along her skull like a clamp tightening.

A strangled gasp escaped her lips. For an instant, she registered the expressions of onlookers. Startled, curious, or holding up phones to record. Then her knees gave way. She plummeted to the carpet, her head spinning so wildly that she hardly felt the impact.

The overhead string lights seemed to pulse. She lay on her side, arms trembling. Her head throbbed in pulses of red and white. She tried to focus on the patterns of the carpet, but the colors smeared together. She heard raised voices, tinged with alarm. The floor felt rough under her cheek, scuffing her skin. She was dimly aware that her body shook in a series of small convulsions she could not stop.

Somewhere above her, Robin's voice rang out, closer now. "Back away, let her breathe!" They pushed through the onlookers, kneeling by Ivy's side. She felt Robin's palm against her shoulder, warm and firm. "Ivy, can you hear me?" they asked, voice taut with fear.

Ivy tried to speak but managed only a ragged breath. The thrumming in her skull magnified, drowning out the drumming from across the hall. Her mouth twisted as she tried to form words. The convulsions subsided into a faint trembling. She forced her eyes to refocus, but the chaos in her vision refused to settle.

The woman in the shawl hovered near Robin, whispering nervously. "She... she saw something. We were just talking and she... oh God, I don't know what happened."

"Give her space," Robin hissed. "Someone call for help!"

A bystander's frantic cry rose above the chatter. "Calling 911!"

Ivy's hearing wavered. She fought to ground herself, inhaling deep, shaky breaths. *Focus on something physical. Focus on Robin's hand.* But the pain flared again, stabbing just behind her eyes. She saw glimmers. The same bridge, a child's terrified face, torn from safety by a churning current. It felt too overwhelming. She wanted to cry out, but her body refused. Darkness tugged at the corners of her sight.

"You're all right," Robin said, leaning close. Their voice faltered. "Stay with me. Keep looking at me."

People crowded around them in a circle, some with phones held up. Through the confusion, Ivy picked out a few gasps, speculation about a seizure or a mental breakdown. She wanted to correct them, to say she was not losing her mind.

Robin pressed their hand gently to Ivy's forehead. "Ivy. Talk to me."

Ivy managed to part her lips, but only a ragged exhale escaped. She felt drenched in sweat. Her heart hammered, and her mouth tasted bitter. She heard the frantic drumbeats again, or maybe that was just her pulse.

Another wave of blackness rippled through her. She tried to fight it, scrabbling for Robin's wrist. "I... the water," she croaked, voice raw. "Bridge... a girl... in the water..."

Robin's anxious face blurred, then sharpened. "What are you seeing? Ivy... you gotta breathe."

She squeezed her eyelids shut. The vision flashed again behind her closed eyes. Water, a scream, a hand vanishing beneath tumultuous waves. Her own fear, coiled tight in her chest, threatened to snap. She felt it in her bones. Something terrible was out there, waiting to happen. Or maybe it was happening already. She did not know how the threads of time aligned.

A voice rose above the chaos. "We have paramedics on the way!"

The pounding in her head surged. She coughed, and tears flooded her vision. Plumes of incense drifted overhead, intensifying the heaviness in her lungs. Everything smelled thick, like cloves and desperation. She caught a phantom taste of salt on her tongue. The dizziness redoubled.

Robin tried to cradle her head. "We'll get you out of here in a second," they murmured. "You're safe."

The word *safe* lodged in Ivy's hazy mind. She was not safe from her own visions. The moment she thought she might still them, they roared back, unstoppable. She tried to breathe again, but her body was too sluggish to cooperate. Her eyelids fluttered, fighting to remain open. The fair around her seemed to recede into blackness.

She felt heat, a deep feverish flush that pooled at her temples. Her muscles clenched painfully, then loosened. Her limbs no longer obeyed her. She was lying limp against Robin, and her thoughts spiraled into a frantic question. Had she done something to bring this on? Had Cassandra's warnings been right? Ivy faintly registered the paramedics arriving. A flurry of official-sounding voices rose behind her. Yet all of it sounded far away. The stress of the past weeks, the confusion, and this new, horrifying glimpse of a girl on a bridge, all pressed in on her consciousness, blotting out sense. Her vision hazed over. She was drifting. Something akin to a whisper brushed against her thoughts. The voice was neither male nor female, more like a presence that curled around the raw edges of her mind. The words reverberated inside her, distinct and certain. *You're waking up too fast.*

She tried to respond, or at least to understand. But darkness closed in, swallowing her in one swift tide. Her last fleeting sensation was the frantic drumbeat of her heart, and Robin desperately calling her name, drowned out by a single final echo. *You're waking up too fast.*

CHAPTER

TEN

THE LETTER

Ivy closed the shop early. Fatigue pressed on her shoulders as the late-afternoon light slanted through the drawn blinds, leaving the interior of The Oracle bathed in a dusky glow. Normally, the warmth of candles and the familiar scent of sandalwood and lavender comforted her, but today every shadow felt like a lurking question she could not answer. The single pot of chamomile tea on her small counter had gone cold. She remained hunched on a wooden stool, gazing at the locked door.

Ever since she collapsed at the metaphysical fair a few days ago, she had been sidestepping texts from curious acquaintances and ignoring calls from old clients. Robin had insisted she take a break, but "rest" felt impossible when her mind churned endlessly with half-formed images. Wobbling shapes in water, a name erased by time that rang louder than any question. Staying open for business now felt fraudulent. She exhaled unsteadily. The overhead lamp buzzed, deepening her headache. She rubbed her temples and forced her attention onto small tasks. Reorganizing a shelf of tarot decks, wiping dusty corners. She wanted to feel grounded, anchor her restless thoughts to something tangible. No matter how she tried, her anxiety refused to loosen its grip.

Late dusk arrived sooner than expected. Pale moonlight filtered through the cracks around the blinds, and the city's murmur shifted into a quieter lull. Ivy lingered by the door, hands pressed to the old wood. She hated how jumpy she felt. Cassandra's voice nagged in the back of her mind, reminding her not to let fear cloud her decisions. Ivy still remembered the fair, the ring of onlookers capturing her collapse on their phones, the feeling of being consumed by too many visions she could not control. Movement on the sidewalk startled her. She peered through the blinds, heart skipping a beat. Someone, tall, shoulders tense, stood outside, scanning the storefront. The figure's posture and messy hair were unmistakable. Ethan. The mix of annoyance and relief that coursed through her made her knees weaken. He had texted a few times, his messages split between worry and that guarded, persistent curiosity he never seemed to shake.

Something in his stance told her he was carrying more than just a notepad this time. He clutched a cream-colored envelope in one hand. Her chest tightened in apprehension. She stepped back from the window, holding her breath. Maybe if she stood still, he would leave. But a decisive knock rattled the glass. And another.

"Ivy? I know you're in there," he called, voice subdued but insistent. "We need to talk."

She closed her eyes, a queasy feeling in her stomach. She disliked how he phrased that, as if conversation were a duty. Yet ignoring him felt impossible. She inhaled and reached for the lock. The handle was cold beneath her palm. When she opened the door a crack, Ethan's gaze locked onto her face. Tension lay coiled in the set of his jaw. He pressed the envelope against his chest.

"I'm closing," she said softly, not meeting his eyes.

"I can see that." He glanced over her shoulder. "But I have something you need to see."

Silence draped between them. The streetlamp behind him glinted, outlining the sharp lines of his cheeks.

He cleared his throat. "I got a letter at work today," he said. "Might be nothing. Might be everything."

She held the door slightly ajar. "I'm really not..."

He cut across her words. "Please. I think it's about you. Or... one of you." He seemed to catch himself, frowning.

At that, she stiffened. She pulled the door open just enough so he could slip inside. The moment he crossed the threshold, she closed and locked it again. He stood awkwardly by the display of tumbled crystals, scanning the subdued interior lit by a single low-watt lamp near the register. Her spool of unused burgundy cloth lay unrolled across the main table, alongside a few journals she had barely glanced at. The shop smelled faintly of old incense and something heavier, like a mixture of tension and stale fear.

"I guess you closed early," he said. His voice was careful, lacking its usual quick-edged curiosity. He shifted the envelope to his other hand. "Here."

Ivy watched warily as he extended it. The envelope was cream-colored, sealed with a dab of wax that had been broken. She noticed the extremely neat handwriting across the front. There was no address, no name. The only sign of origin was a faint, embossed shape pressed into the wax, some kind of raven or crow silhouette, partially torn.

"What is this?" she asked, not yet taking it.

He exhaled. "It was in the newsroom's mail stack this morning. I was sorting through junk, bills, press releases. Then I saw this. No return address, just the phrase 'Confidential: E. Matson.' Figured it might be from a tipster. But inside..." He gestured for her to read.

She swallowed the knot in her throat and lifted out a single piece of cream-colored paper. The writing was spare, a spidery script in black ink.

To the true Seer. It's not her.
Signed,
L. Rivers

A chill snaked up her spine. The words resonated with an accusatory note. She read them again, taking in every curve of the letters. She had never heard of L. Rivers.

"It's not her," she echoed softly. Her fingers dug into the edges of the paper. "What does that mean?"

Ethan raked a hand through his hair. "I have no idea. I

searched online...rummaged through old city records. No hits for that phrase. No results for an L. Rivers."

The letter rustled in her trembling hold. "So, you thought you should show me." She forced a small, bitter laugh. "Looks like someone's out there bragging about a 'true Seer'... and apparently, I'm not it."

He stepped closer. Her pulse hammered at the proximity.

"Maybe you were right," he said quietly. "About me lying to myself. About all the times I asked for proof but refused to see what was in front of me. I can't ignore letters like this anymore. Not after what happened... with you. The meltdown at the fair. The BART station. I keep running into signs that there's more going on."

Ivy's chest tightened. She did not want to recall the meltdown. She could still feel the sting of her knees hitting the carpet, the blur of onlookers. She also did not want to offer him the reassurance he seemed to seek.

Quietly, she asked, "You think this letter is telling you I'm... not genuine?" She shoved the paper back inside the envelope. "You never believed me anyway. So why does it matter?"

He pressed his lips into a thin line. "Maybe it matters because you do. And I..." He inhaled. "I might believe you more than I ever let on."

Her throat constricted. She did not know if she should feel angry or relieved at that admission. She pressed the envelope to her sternum. "That's not a real answer."

"This letter suggests we might be dealing with deeper networks than the local news can handle. People who claim to know something about seers. You. Why else send it to me?"

She shook her head, tears prickling at the corners of her eyes. She did not want to care about cryptic strangers mailing ominous notes. She wanted to hide under blankets and let the world spin on. But the letter burned in her hand. She felt singled out, targeted.

"Ivy... hey." Ethan's voice softened. He reached out, brushing reluctant fingertips over her forearm. She flinched, but he did not retreat. "Whatever it means, I had to tell you. I needed you to know you're being spoken about. Maybe threatened, maybe discredited. I don't know. But this is real."

She stared at the envelope, her eyes clouding. "I never asked for any of this," she whispered. "I sure didn't ask to be singled out by mysterious letters. I already feel... like I can't keep up." Her voice caught.

The overhead lamp blinked. "I know it's not fair," Ethan said. "But you can't look at me and say it doesn't concern you."

She did not respond. Instead, she reread the words. *To the true Seer. It's not her.* She felt a spike of anger, then a flood of confusion. If she was not "her," who was she? For so long, she had wrestled with the question of whether her visions made her special or cursed. Now, evidently, someone out there had decided she was neither, merely a stand-in for something else.

Her words emerged in a measured whisper. "Then who the hell am I?"

Ethan frowned at the raw note in her voice. He tried to

speak, but she cut him off by turning abruptly toward the door. Her heart hammered. She could not endure his well-meaning gaze any longer. Without a second thought, she grabbed the handle and wrenched it open, the doorframe rattling from the force. She turned back to him, meeting his startled eyes. "That's all I can handle tonight," she said, voice wavering. "I can't do this. I'm sorry."

His eyes darted with an urgency that bordered on panic. "Ivy, wait. I..."

She slammed the door, the impact vibrating through her palm. In the silence that followed, she heard her heartbeat pulsing in her ears. Part of her wanted to fling the door open and beg him to stay. But bitterness, wounded pride, and confusion jumbled too fiercely. He knocked again, an uneasy tap that almost crumpled the wall of her resolve. She bit down on her lip, forcing herself to remain quiet. She felt tears trailing down her cheeks, but her jaw stayed clenched, determined.

"Ivy," he called out softly. "Please."

His plea hung in the dark. Her hand hovered over the knob. But she stood as still as possible, breathing in shallow, ragged pulls. Finally, his footsteps shuffled away, slow and reluctant. She waited until she heard them fade. An ache travelled through her chest, and she realized she still clutched that envelope in her trembling fingers. The words inside pulsed in her mind. An accusation, a dismissal, a chilling challenge all at once.

CHAPTER

ELEVEN

THE INVESTIGATION

Ivy sat on the edge of her living room couch, trying to concentrate on an unread journal balanced in her lap. Candlelight glimmered across the walls, but the usual comfort felt distant tonight. She thumbed the corner of the worn leather cover. Her eyes drifted to her phone, which sat silent and face-down on the coffee table. She had ignored three texts from Ethan earlier. Each message was short, all circling the same question. Could she explain why Cassandra's name appeared in old police records.

Ivy had read his words more than once, her heart pounding. She had no immediate answers. Her aunt had always been guarded about her past. Ivy did not know if the mystery around Cassandra stemmed from personal heartbreak, involvement with other psychics, or something more troubling.

Anxious curiosity finally won. She flipped over her phone again. No new notifications. Sighing, she set the journal aside. Too many thoughts made her restless. She missed the time when normal business hours ended and she could lock the door to The Oracle, confident that her day's problems would not follow her home. Lately, life bled from one hour into the next. Visions, cryptic threats, and the reporter who refused to back away from mysteries he could not prove, it all tangled into a single knot in her chest. She wanted to unravel it but had no idea where to start.

Fresh air, she decided. She stood and crossed to the window. Outside, a stretch of fog draped the dark street. She wondered if Ethan was hunched over his computer somewhere, scouring public archives for any mention of Cassandra Vale. Her hunch was correct. At half past midnight, her phone vibrated once. Ethan's name lit the screen.

This time, she answered.

"Ivy," he said. She heard a rustle of papers in the background.

She held her breath. "Yeah?"

"I know it's late. I'm sorry," he said. She sensed fierce focus beneath his patient tone. "I found something about your aunt, and I need to talk."

She sank back into the couch, holding the phone tight. "Found what, exactly?"

His exhale crackled through the line. "She's connected to a defunct psychic group from years ago, the Seer's Circle. It was investigated by the SFPD. The local records mention 'Vale' multiple times, but the details in the file are sealed. I'm guessing Cassandra was..."

"Stop," Ivy said, her voice hoarse. "Let me try to call her. If you want answers, maybe you can get them face to face. She can decide what she'll share."

Ivy expected him to bristle. Instead, he paused, with a faint clink of dishware on his end of the call. "She invited me to come by tomorrow," he said. "I assume she plans to talk or at least set me straight about something. I figured you should know."

Ivy's stomach tightened. "You're meeting her tomorrow?" Cassandra seldom welcomed strangers. That she had agreed to speak with Ethan hinted at her deeper concern. "Are you going alone?"

"Yes. Unless you want to be there."

She glanced at the scattered notes and half-burned candles on her living room table. "I'm not sure how she'd feel about that," Ivy said slowly. "She might clam up if both of us show up."

"You might be right," Ethan allowed. "Just... stay reachable, in case I need help sorting out what she says. I have a feeling this story runs deeper than any of us realized."

His words summoned a chill. "All right. Good luck." She ended the call and set the phone down. Sleep felt impossible.

The next day, Ivy left her shop early. She found it impossible to concentrate there, where every shuffle of a tarot deck reminded her that she had few answers for her own predicament, let alone her clients. Getting ahead of her mounting tension felt hopeless, so she headed directly for her aunt's townhouse in Nob Hill. The cable car line rattled in the distance, carrying office workers and tourists up the steep incline.

She arrived on Cassandra's block just before dusk. Gilded lamplight illuminated the ornate doorknobs and carved lintels of the old Victorian houses lining the street. She knocked lightly on Cassandra's heavy wooden door. No immediate answer. The ivy that clung to the townhouse's exterior stretched across the window frames. Ivy brushed a tendril aside and peered through the narrow glass pane. The entry hall was shadowy, but she saw a single lamp shining at the far end.

"Aunt Cass?" she called. She tried the doorknob. To her surprise, it turned easily. She stepped inside and closed the door behind her. The lingering odor of old incense and sage tickled her nose. Cassandra appeared at the far end of the hall, her long skirts sweeping the floor.

"Ivy. I meant to leave the door locked," she said. She did not sound annoyed, only resigned. "But you're expected."

Ivy swallowed. "I know Ethan's coming. I wanted to see if you needed me here."

Cassandra studied her face. "Did he send you?"

"No. I came on my own."

A faint shadow crossed Cassandra's features. It could have been relief, or worry, or a blend of both. She gestured with a slight tilt of her head, guiding Ivy down the hallway. They entered the living room, a cluttered but elegant space thick with layers of candle wax, dusty mirrored trays, and stacked books. Cassandra directed Ivy to an armchair near the tall windows. "He's not due for another half hour," she said. "I appreciate the concern, but I know how to talk to a reporter."

Ivy sank into the chair. "He's not simply a reporter anymore," she said softly. "He knows things I never told him. He's been digging into your past, your name... he found some kind of old police file. I'm worried he'll push you too hard."

She watched Cassandra's expression carefully. Her aunt poured tea into two delicate cups, handed one to Ivy, and kept the other. The porcelain clinked as Cassandra set the teapot aside. "That depends on what he thinks he knows."

"He mentioned a secret society," Ivy said. "The Seer's Circle. He said you were a part of it, and that it was investigated for something serious."

Cassandra pressed her lips into a thin line. "There are many things I've left unsaid. For your sake and mine." She hesitated. "That group... we used to meet quietly in the city, focusing on advanced techniques and illusions. It ended badly."

Footsteps outside the house ended the conversation. Cassandra's gaze moved toward the door. "I'll speak to him alone," Cassandra said. "If you stay, be invisible." She downed what was left of her tea. "Curiosity is a hunger, and well-fed curiosity can devour caution. Do not let him devour yours."

Ivy rose from the chair as Cassandra walked to the entry hall. She found a corner near a tall bookshelf where she could stay out of sight but still hear. She slid behind it, anxious to watch the exchange. She cradled her teacup, trying not to rattle it with her trembling hands.

Ethan's footsteps sounded on the porch. A knock followed. Cassandra answered. "You are hardly punctual," she remarked. "Though I suppose you needed time to gather your nerve."

Ivy craned her neck. She saw Ethan standing in the threshold, wearing a slightly wrinkled jacket. He carried a few folded sheets of paper. He cleared his throat. "I appreciate you seeing me," he said, voice steady. "I'm eager to confirm some things about a group you were involved with. The official records list you as a key member of the Seer's Circle."

Cassandra moved aside, letting him enter. She led him into the living room. Ethan stood near the doorway, back stiff, as though bracing for an argument. From Ivy's vantage, she could see how his knuckles whitened around his stack of files.

"You look pale," Cassandra said calmly. "Come, put those papers down before you tear them in half."

Ethan obeyed, setting his notes on a side table. "I found mention of your psychic group in the city archives," he said. "The name 'Vale' shows up multiple times. A few references to a caretaker's testimony, but no formal statements from you. The entire file is sealed, but it reads like everyone involved vanished without explanation after the SFPD started looking into you."

Cassandra did not reply at first. She lit a candle with the practiced flick of a match. Light wavered across her face, underscoring the cool precision in her eyes.

"Curiosity is a hunger," she said, repeating the phrase she had told Ivy. "But be careful what you feed it, Mr. Matson. Some histories refuse to stay buried."

Ivy watched Ethan's Adam's apple bob. "I can't ignore what I've seen, not after recent events," he said. "I want to understand how it all connects. I found the sealed police file. It's flagged for 'suspicious activity' and 'dangerous practices.' The report mentions financial misconduct and manipulative rituals. Your name is all over it, Cassandra. What was that group doing?"

Cassandra set the match aside. "Why ask me? The city is full of secrets. If you chase one, you might stumble into a hundred more."

Ethan stepped closer. "My job is to chase secrets. Right now, one answer leads me directly here." His eyes moved to the books stacked in precarious columns. "What do you know about the original Seer's Circle?"

At that question, Cassandra fell silent. The living room felt unnervingly still. Ivy held her breath. She knew her aunt well enough to see the subtle shift in her shoulders.

"You say 'Seer's Circle' as though it's a myth," Cassandra said at last, her voice quiet. "Why should I offer an explanation to a stranger who does not know what he's asking?"

Ethan let a faint, awkward laugh escape, though it did not quite reach his eyes. "Because Ivy might be at risk," he replied. "Because the more I pull at these threads, your name, a secret society, cryptic references to prophecies, the more I worry that someone is hunting her, or you, or both."

Cassandra's fingers tightened around the unlit candles on the mantel. "Hunting? I doubt there is any single hunter, Mr. Matson. This city is a labyrinth of overlapping motives." Her gaze slid toward the corner of the room where Ivy stood hidden. Ivy's heart stuttered, but Cassandra did not betray her presence. Instead, she glanced back at Ethan. "You should have rung the doorbell sooner, so I could blow the dust off my secrets before you demanded them."

Candlelight glinted on Ethan's face. The tension pressed at Ivy's lungs.

Ethan inhaled slowly. "I'm not here to cause trouble. But I won't stop pursuing the truth."

"That much is clear," Cassandra said.

He indicated at the files he had placed on the table. "I keep finding these references to illusions, circle gatherings, old correspondences. I suspect you might have led or been part of a psychic group that was investigated for its dangerous practices. Whatever that group was, it sounds eerily connected to what Ivy's experiencing."

Cassandra remained as immovable as stone, her eyes reflecting the candle's glow. For a moment, Ivy believed her aunt would dismiss Ethan outright. But she set the candles aside and faced him. "I have no statement to make on the record," she said, voice stiff. "I do not plan to relive the past, no matter how intensely you pry. If Ivy's well-being concerns you, protect her in the present. Digging through old bones will only rattle them."

The silence deepened. Ethan gave a slow nod, though frustration edged his posture. He glanced at Cassandra's resolute face and must have realized he would get nothing more tonight. He cleared his throat, letting the tension rest.

Cassandra turned away first, crossing to the window. She gripped the edge of the thick velvet curtain that hung to the sill. Outside, the last of the day's light faded into the city's brimming dusk. Ivy saw how the lines around her aunt's eyes drew tighter.

Ethan took one step back. "I appreciate the invitation," he said, though he seemed disappointed by how little had been revealed. "If you ever change your mind about sharing the truth, you know where to find me."

Cassandra said nothing.

He gathered his files, tucking them back under his arm. With a final, lingering glance at Cassandra, he headed toward the hallway. Ivy watched him vanish from her line of sight, footsteps muffled by the thick carpet. A moment later, as the door closed with a click, she resisted the urge to chase after him.

Cassandra stood still, her posture firm. Ivy took a tentative step out from behind the bookshelf.

"Aunt Cass?" Ivy asked softly. "Are you all right?"

She did not turn. "The original Seer's Circle," she said, her voice low. "He asked about it so calmly, as though it were a footnote in an old textbook. That alone tells me how much he doesn't understand."

Ivy opened her mouth to reply, but Cassandra's words cut the quiet. "He's feeding his curiosity half-truths and rumors." She let the corner of the curtain fall, her hand trembling against the fabric. "That can be dangerous for all of us."

Ivy ventured closer. "He mentioned he's worried about me, about someone targeting us. Is he wrong?"

Cassandra turned her head slightly. "I can't say." She paused, lips parted as though searching for the right phrase. "I do know that certain parts of the past remain locked away for good reason. And if he tries to resurrect them..."

She trailed off. Ivy walked behind her aunt, glancing at the candlelight dancing along the windowsill. She understood the weight of Cassandra's unspoken fear. Revelations about the old circle might explain some of Ivy's struggles, but they could also open the door to new dangers.

Cassandra inhaled and squared her shoulders. "Go home, Ivy," she said. "You saw how disappointed he was. He won't let this go, but for now, his questions must remain unanswered."

Ivy nodded, though unease turned her stomach. She realized that while Ethan had left with hollow hands, he would keep digging. A faint guilt tugged at her heart. He only wanted to protect her, even if his approach could tear open old wounds.

Cassandra extinguished the candle on the mantel with a quick pinch. She turned to face Ivy fully. "That is enough for tonight," Cassandra said softly. "He asked about the original Seer's Circle, and my silence was answer enough."

She expelled a breath, and the glow of the living room seemed to dim as though it shared her resignation. Ivy swallowed, realizing that no matter how many times she demanded clarity, Cassandra intended to keep much locked away. She realized, too, that Ethan had confronted her aunt with a steeled determination that would not vanish.

Ivy stared into the remnants of the candle's glow, unsettled by the truth that none of them yet knew how this puzzle fit together. She set her teacup on a nearby table, turning to gather her coat from the hall. Her mind spun with a jumble of fears. Cassandra stood rooted in that faint circle of light, unyielding. Her eyes reflected a knowledge Ivy still did not share, even as they filled with unspoken warning. Ethan's question hung in the air, unresolved. Cassandra's silence was answer enough, and a warning.

TWELVE

THE INTERVIEW II

Ivy hovered near the display shelf in her shop, straightening brass incense holders for the fourth time that afternoon. The Oracle had reopened a week ago, and though she had dusted every corner, the place still felt tense. The faint smell of sage lingered near the curtained doorway, while a single lamp illuminated the tarot reading table. Shadows cast by the flame of the candle danced across jars of polished crystals, throwing faint rainbows onto the teal walls.

She swallowed against the dryness in her throat. Usually, this late in the day, she would be winding down. Closing the register, counting tea-light candles with the last bit of incense smoke wafting out the front door. Today, though, she could hardly keep focus. She kept picturing Ethan stepping inside again, and her stomach twisted. Her phone chimed, a quiet ping that echoed too loudly. It was Robin. A short text checking in. Ivy set the phone aside. She wanted to answer. She also wanted to turn it off. She felt adrenaline coil in her chest whenever she remembered the note Ethan had shown her.

For a moment, she busied herself by taking a stack of faded Tarot decks from the shelf, verifying each was complete. Her fingertips brushed the well-worn paper. A wave of nostalgia lapped at her, recalling a time when she used these decks mechanically, only half-nodding at the possibility that her visions might be real. Now, that naive distance was gone.

Footsteps sounded outside, slow and measured. Her pulse kicked. She turned toward the window, seeing a familiar silhouette approach, a tall man with broad shoulders. He paused at the threshold, then rapped on the doorframe. The glass shook softly. Ivy inhaled and crossed the room. She pulled the door open, ignoring the cold air from outside. Ethan stood there, wearing a gray button-down that looked half rumpled, his hair unkempt as usual. She could tell he was short on sleep. His gaze carried a quiet intensity that made her heart jolt.

"Hi," he said, voice subdued. He peered past her into the shop. "You're open."

"I am," she said. She settled on a stiff nod. "Come in, I guess."

He came forward, letting the door swing shut. The bell overhead gave a forlorn tinkle. She noticed he still clutched an off-white envelope, the same one she had seen before. Her heart thumped at the memory of the words scrawled inside. *To the true Seer. It's not her.*

Silence stretched, punctuated only by a car horn somewhere down the block. Ethan cleared his throat. He approached the main table where she did readings, placing the envelope and his notebook side by side.

She folded her arms and mustered a steady voice. "Why did you come back?"

He exhaled, casting a quick glance around the shop. The overhead lights caught the faint gold in his eyes. "Because someone doesn't think you're the real deal." He tapped the envelope. "And neither do I," he added, though his tone sounded less certain than the words implied. "But I can't ignore what I saw. My confusion, my skepticism, none of it matters if the things you've predicted keep coming true."

Heat saturated low in her stomach. "Let's pretend I believe you're here out of concern," she said quietly. "Where does that leave us?"

He shifted, nodding toward the letter. "It leaves us with evidence that someone else is making declarations about you, this L. Rivers person. I need to know why they're so sure."

"It's not exactly a compliment," she replied, her voice tight. "And your presence here... I don't get it. You spent so long doubting me. Now you're half convinced, but you show up with that insulting note anyway?"

"I'm not convinced," he shot back, then paused, realising that he sounded defensive. He lowered his voice. "I'm unsettled. Something is happening with you, around you, that normal explanations can't cover. I can't lie to myself about it anymore."

She studied him a moment, then slowly exhaled. There was a faint tangle of sympathy twisting beneath her anger. He was not entirely sure of anything, yet he chose to be here. She gestured for him to sit at the table and took a seat opposite.

"All right, so we talk," she said. "What do you want to know?"

He sat at the table, gripping the edge of the envelope. "Tell me about your meltdown at the fair. What did you see? What triggered it?"

She pressed her lips into a tight line. "I touched some-one's hand during a reading. I got bombarded with... images I wasn't prepared for. It was overwhelming. I blacked out."

"Like the BART accident?" he asked.

She nodded, shoulders tense. "Similar but not quite. The BART vision was specific, a single moment in time. The fair meltdown was like a hundred little shards of possibility, all trying to punch through at once."

His pen scratched faintly over his notebook. "And you couldn't separate them?"

"No. They blurred." She moved her gaze to the candle near them. "It's not always easy to interpret what I see. Which is why this letter," she tapped the envelope point-edly, "scares me. If multiple vantage points exist, if I'm not who I think I am, what do I do with these visions?"

He opened the envelope, sliding out the note. Ivy caught sight of the bold black handwriting. *To the true Seer. It's not her.* Beneath it, the signature was an elegant *L. Rivers.* He pointed to it. "I found no consistent records on that name. If it's a pseudonym, they're good at covering their tracks."

Her throat felt suddenly dry. "It implies there's someone else. That I'm just... an impostor?"

Ethan rested his hand over the note, concern crossing his features. "It could be a threat. Or a test. I don't know. What I do know is that half the time, I still question everything about you. But I can't run from the facts. You predicted something no one else could have known."

A shiver went through her. She could not help remembering the chilly sidewalk when she first met him, the day he stood outside the police station, listening as the officer brushed her off. A thousand small collisions had happened since, fracturing her sense of a normal life. Now he was sitting in front of her, not as a disbelieving reporter, but as a man caught in the same questions.

"What are you suggesting?" she asked. Her voice wavered.

He took a long moment to reply, flipping his notebook shut. "If you're not the real Seer, we're dealing with two possibilities. This other person is out there, and maybe they want you out of the way. Or they think you're overshadowing them. Or maybe," his tone turned grim, "this is about discrediting you before your visions can reveal something more significant."

She tried to swallow the knot in her throat. "I never asked to reveal anything," she said softly. "I didn't want this."

He studied her for a beat, eyes softening. "I know," he said. "But we can't make it disappear by pretending it's not real."

She glanced away, fixing her gaze on a tiny crack in the

tabletop. Tension charged the air between them. She felt the memory of his last visit, how she slammed the door, the way confusion and hurt tangled in her chest afterward.

He reached for the letter. "The part that haunts me... is that we keep circling around your authenticity. The letter claims there is a different 'true Seer.' That means something deeper is going on. It's not about you making headlines or me writing a story. We're in a bigger mess, and you might be in danger."

She dragged her focus back to him. He was worried, she realized, though he tried to mask it well. The realization loosened something in her chest. The annoyance she carried at his skepticism cracked, letting a fragile gratitude seep through.

"And if I'm in danger... do you plan to keep digging?" she asked.

His lips pressed together. "Yes. Because I can't shake the feeling that you're connected to a chain of events we haven't begun to unravel. And because, in the end, you might need someone to stand in your corner, whether you want me there or not."

Her heart thudded. It would be so simple to push him away. But that would leave her alone with the letter, alone with the visions. She remembered how it felt not having anyone believe in her.

"You're not the only one antsy for answers," she said, letting out a shaky breath. "I can't keep waiting around for the next letter or some cryptic sign. But I don't know where to start."

He rested his elbows on the table, leaning in slightly. The interplay of lamplight made his eyes look almost gold. "We start with the simplest question," he said. "If you're not the 'true Seer'... who is?"

Ivy's pulse fluttered. She tried to imagine a nameless person lurking somewhere, sending notes, sowing doubt. The possibility both stung and frightened her. Her lip trembled. "Then who is the 'true Seer'?" she whispered. "And what am I?"

Ethan set the note aside. The tension in his frame eased slightly, and his voice dropped low. "Maybe the better question is, what are we getting into?"

For a moment, Ivy felt all the anger, the lingering mistrust, the tangled anxiety knotting her insides. Yet she could also sense the faint glow of something else between them, a promise that they might face the unknown together. She inhaled, trying to steady the accelerated beat of her heart.

She opened her mouth, uncertain what to say. Before any answer could form, she felt the warmth of his eyes on her face, urging her to trust him, at least in this precarious moment. The candle on the table fluttered once. What are they getting into?

And she knew neither of them had the full answer. Not yet.

CHAPTER

THIRTEEN

THE FIRE

I vy lay awake, staring at the patterns on her bedroom ceiling. She had tried to doze off for hours, but leftover adrenaline would not let her sink into sleep. A single candle glimmered on the small table near her window, casting jittery shapes across the walls. The subtle fragrance of lavender and sage drifted in the room, meant to calm her, yet her nerves buzzed.

She had texted Ethan earlier, a short message to see if he was safe. He did not respond, and a hollowness spread in her chest at the thought of him out there, digging around for evidence about her aunt's past. He was so certain that the truth lingered somewhere in old archives and half-forgotten testimonies. The intensity in his eyes had left her unsettled. She could not forget his words. He would keep hunting answers no matter where they led. She rolled onto her side, hoping the shift in position would lull her mind, but the attempt was futile. Frustration pounded in her temples. An image of Ethan's jacket, rumpled at the sleeves, clicked in her thoughts like a persistent metronome. The memory stirred an unwelcome ache. Worry laced with something more complicated, something that felt too large and dangerous to name.

A soft, muffled snore from the living room reminded her she was not alone. Robin had insisted on crashing on the couch, unwilling to let her spend the night by herself. They had a knack for bringing a quiet steadiness, a friendship that felt as solid as stone. Ivy rubbed her arms briskly, trying to dispel a sudden chill. She closed her eyes, counting backward from ten, urging her brain to shut off. It happened so quickly that she did not register the moment she dozed. One second, she was bathed in candlelight, the next she was somewhere else.

Heat rushed at her in a wild gust. She was surrounded by what felt like the scorching interior of a furnace. Every breath scalded her lungs. Her eyes stung from waves of shimmering red-orange light. She turned in frantic circles, searching for the source of the blaze, and she saw him. Ethan stood behind a barricade of glass, its smooth surface streaked with soot. He pounded on the wall, his voice trapped behind the inferno. Flames licked around his silhouette, turning every angle of his face into sharp, terror-stricken lines. She could almost see the sweat breaking across his brow, the panic glinting in his eyes as he shouted something her ears could not register. She could only watch, powerless, as the flames surged higher, crackling with predatory glee.

Time felt sludgy, stretched thin by horror. She tried to run for him, tried to slam her palm to the glass to break it.

Her arm moved as if weighed by chains. The flame devoured the world in burning brightness. She thought she heard his voice calling her name, raw and desperate, before the vision shattered. Her scream tore her back into her bedroom. She shot upright, lungs burning as if the smoke had followed her. The candle on the table moved wildly from her sudden movement. She pressed a trembling hand to her chest, trying to breathe.

Soft footfalls approached. The narrow rectangle of light from the hallway tufted at her bedroom door, and Robin burst in, eyes wide and hair messy from sleep. "Ivy?" they breathed. Their voice was filled with worry as they switched the overhead lamp on. "Hey, I'm here. What happened?"

Ivy struggled to speak. Her heart hammered like it wanted to break free from her ribs. "It was him," she rasped. "I saw him burning."

They did not ask who she meant. They already knew. Robin closed the distance in a quick stride, climbing onto the edge of Ivy's bed to place a supporting arm around her shoulders. Ivy leaned into that quiet comfort, fighting the tears that threatened. She stared at the bedside candle, as if it might leap into a wide inferno at any moment.

"Talk to me," Robin said with gentle insistence.

Ivy inhaled deeply, trying to gather pieces of her scattered mind. "I was asleep, although it happened so fast, I couldn't tell if it was a real dream or a vision." A tremor shuddered through her. "I saw Ethan... behind glass. A wall or a barrier. Flames everywhere. I couldn't reach him, and he was calling my name."

Robin's brows drew together in concern. "You're sure it was a vision?"

The memory of the scorching air still clung to Ivy's skin. "I'm sure," she said, voice cracking. "It felt real. The heat, the way the fire sounded like it was hungry." She closed her eyes, but the image of Ethan's wide, terrified gaze seared her.

Robin took hold of Ivy's hand, their thumb rubbing slow circles on her palm. They glanced at the half-burned candle and quietly pinched the wick, plunging the room into shadow aside from the mild overhead light. "Then we need to tell him," they said softly. "We can't let him walk around with no idea he might be in danger. If your vision is a warning, we're letting him stumble right into it."

Ivy wanted to argue, but no words formed. The idea of telling Ethan about the fire tugged at a knot in her stomach. If she warned him, would it become inevitable? Every time she shared a vision, the outcomes seemed to rush toward them, as if naming the threat gave it permission to manifest. She glanced at Robin, her throat too tight to voice these thoughts.

The urge to stay silent, to not speak the vision into existence, warred with the memory of Ethan's terrified face seared behind her eyes. Every instinct she possessed screamed that the fire was not a metaphor or a distant possibility. It was a hungry, imminent threat. Robin's firm insistence that they had to warn him only solidified the choice already forming in Ivy's gut. Calling him was out of the question. The time wasted on his logical questions and skepticism was a luxury she could not afford. No, she could not just warn him. She had to get to him.

A fragment of a previously overheard conversation suddenly clicked into place with chilling clarity. Ethan had mentioned a meeting with a whistleblower, someone tied to the Seer's Circle, somewhere near Pier 47. Propelled by a scorching urgency that eclipsed her own fear, Ivy raced out into the late afternoon, her heart pounding with each step she took along the waterfront road. The journey across the city to the gloomy, rust-streaked warehouses was a torment of rising panic, the phantom crackle of fire and the imagined scent of smoke clinging to her senses as she hunted for the building, driven by the one, singular dread that she might already be too late.

Ivy stood in the cold, gripping her phone so tightly that her knuckles ached. Her senses buzzed with the same scorching urgency she had felt in her dream. The crackle of potential fire, the stifling press of heat, and Ethan's face contorted with fear. She hated how much this vision clung to her. Even now, her heart pounded with each step she took along the waterfront road. The warehouses here formed a gloomy row, their rust-streaked exteriors illuminated only by the dim glow of overhead lamps. She guessed Ethan was inside one of them, chasing a lead.

She had debated telling him about her premonition. He would have asked a thousand questions she could not answer. Instead, she relied on instinct. She had overheard him mention the meeting and had gleaned enough detail to discern the location. A derelict building near the Pier, left to rot by owners who could not afford renovations or demolitions. She spotted the correct warehouse by a hunch, the second structure from the corner, with broken windows taped unevenly from the inside. An old wooden sign read "Bay Shipping Co." The sign hung crooked, swaying in a light breeze that smelled of brine and engine fumes. She ran her palm across her jittery stomach, steeling her nerves.

She peered at the padlocked gate. The entire fence was bent. A single chain lay on the gravel, flakes of rust marking the spot. Frowning, she jiggled the gate. It opened without effort, and she hurried inside. Tall stacks of rotting pallets and shipping containers lined the perimeter, leaving narrow walkways. The place felt forgotten, a graveyard of old commerce. Ivy shivered at the gloom. Her new challenge was finding a way into the structure. She inched along its length until she spotted a small door near the loading dock. Warm light trickled through the cracked threshold. She pressed her ear against the metal. She sensed movement inside, like a faint echo of footsteps on concrete. She tried the handle, relieved to find it unlocked.

She walked in quietly, adjusting to the dim interior. The ceiling soared overhead, skeletal beams broken in places. Scattered crates made uneven rows along the floor, and old forklift tracks formed ghostly lines in the dust. A pair of fluorescent lamps blinked near an office in the corner. That seemed like the logical place for a clandestine meeting. Ivy moved as silently as she could, slipping behind stacked crates and trying to quell her rising fear. She had no plan, only the pressing dread that Ethan was in danger. She paused behind a rusted dolly, listening. Then she heard voices.

"I told you everything," a man insisted. "All of it was in the ledger. Those records are how the Circle tracked finances, membership, and everything else."

A second voice, warmer, steadier, resonated through the gloom. That was Ethan. "Thank you, Darius. I need to confirm these details. Are you sure no one else has a copy?"

"Positive," Darius replied. "I... kept them hidden. I knew they'd come after me if they found out I was the one who leaked membership lists. Lucien's name came up everywhere. He was the one controlling the hush money."

Ivy's breath caught. *Lucien*, she thought. That name never failed to raise her pulse. She edged closer, peeking around a crate. She saw Ethan's silhouette. He stood near a makeshift table, a damaged metal slab that seemed like it once was part of a shipping conveyor. He wore a gray shirt, sleeves rolled to his elbows, and he clutched his worn leather notebook. Across from him stood Darius Greene, a wiry man with anxious eyes and a rumpled jacket.

"I can't go public," Darius stressed, pushing his glasses up the bridge of his nose. "I revealed enough already. They'll try to silence me."

Ethan nodded solemnly. "I understand. I promise I'll protect your identity."

A broken fluorescent lamp overhead buzzed. Ivy's gaze moved upward, noticing a tangle of exposed wiring hanging near a rusted girder. Something about the darkness up there set her teeth on edge. In the half-shadows, she could have sworn she saw a spark.

She froze. A voice inside her warned that this was the moment from her nightmare. She had not recognized the location in her vision, only the oppressive sense of heat and the sight of Ethan behind a barrier. But now she realized the barrier might be falling debris or fire, not glass. She needed to act. Creeping closer, she opened her mouth to call his name, when another spark crackled across the wiring. The sudden pop made Ethan and Darius look up in alarm. The overhead lamp blinked wildly, then died with a low mechanical hiss. The warehouse sank into gloom.

Ethan's voice rang through, calm but alert. "We should move to the exit, just in…"

A flare of orange light erupted near the girder. Loose wires hissed as electricity arced, and a section of old insulation burst into flames. Smoke trickled upward and thickened with a hungry cloud.

"Get away from there!" Ivy screamed. She forgot caution, bolting forward. "Move, now!"

Ethan whirled, eyes widening as he recognized her voice. Darius looked terrified, dropping a sheaf of papers. Smoke poured downward in ominous waves, and the metal beams groaned as sparks leaped from rafter to rafter.

Ivy rushed to Ethan's side. She grabbed his arm, voice shaking. "We have to leave. It's going to spread."

He stared at her in bewilderment but nodded, casting a quick glance at Darius. "Run for the door," Ethan commanded. "Follow us."

The flames jumped to a ragged corner of the roof, sending embers across the dusty floor. A few crates ignited. The smoke seared Ivy's eyes, and she coughed, shielding her face with her forearm. She half-dragged Ethan around a low stack of boxes as they headed toward the entry door, hoping it was still a viable exit.

Behind them, Darius stumbled, choking. Ivy slowed, wracked with guilt. She had come for Ethan, but she could not abandon Darius. She reached out with her free hand, beckoning him to wrap an arm around her shoulders. Together, the three of them pressed forward. Flames crackled across the overhead beams, and she heard the screech of metal warping in the heat. It sounded like a beast in agony.

"Faster!" Ivy choked. Her lungs burned, and tears blurred her vision. They made it halfway to the door when part of the roof collapsed in a spraying burst of sparks. A wave of cinders showered the floor, splitting them apart. Ivy felt Ethan's grip slip as a chunk of charred wood smashed into the crates nearby, scattering debris. She stumbled, but forced herself upright. Through layers of smoke, she glimpsed Ethan on the other side of the wreckage, coughing. He called her name, voice raw and urgent. Darius crouched beside him, head lowered, arms shielding his face.

Ivy scrambled around the burning fragments, ignoring the way her chest constricted from the smoke. She forced her legs to steady. Another flaming chunk slammed down nearby, shaking the floor. She jumped back with a startled cry and realized the entire center portion of the ceiling was caving in. The exit door behind them stood only a dozen steps away, but new flames licked across the threshold as the building's structure crumbled. Her mind travelled back to that haunting dream. Ethan behind glass, unreachable. Steeling herself, she lunged around a toppled crate, ignoring the sparks that landed on her jacket. She heard a crash above, more beams fracturing.

She spotted Ethan through the haze, eyes streaming. He had flung an arm across Darius's shoulders. Relief surging through her, Ivy gripped Ethan's wrist, pulling him forward. Together, they skidded over twisted metal. Light shone near the far side of the warehouse, a broken overhead door that hung halfway open. Ivy realized it must lead to a loading bay adjacent to the lot. With the main entrance blocked, the bay might be their only chance.

She patted Ethan's arm. "That way!" she shouted above the roar of flames.

They staggered toward the partial exit. Darius stumbled and nearly fell, but Ethan steadied him. Ivy coughed, tasting bitter smoke. The scorching air stung her nostrils. She forced herself to remain focused on that sliver of open space ahead. A loud groan reverberated overhead, deeper, more menacing than before. She saw a flame devour the remains of the roof beam. Lurching sideways, she grabbed Ethan's shoulder again. "We need to hurry!"

A final series of snaps and cracks signaled the beam's total collapse. She glimpsed a massive wedge of wood plummeting down, trailing embers. It crashed behind them, shaking the entire warehouse. Splinters exploded everywhere, clattering on the cement floor. The impact rattled Ivy's bones as she dragged her feet forward, refusing to surrender to the blazing inferno. By the time they reached the half-open loading bay, flames had crawled up most of the walls. The heat wrapped around them like a suffocating cloak. Ethan pried the rusted door open the rest of the way. All three of them scrambled outside onto a cracked concrete ramp. Cold air instantly hit Ivy's cheeks. She and Ethan stumbled down the ramp, supporting Darius, until they reached an abandoned stretch of asphalt. Ivy bent over, coughing violently as she tried to catch her breath. Her throat felt scraped raw. Ethan coughed too, rubbing a hand across his forehead. Darius, hunched and trembling, sank to his knees.

They blinked in the fading daylight, the sky tinged orange from the setting sun. The air smelled of burning plastic and charred wood. Ivy and Ethan took several moments to recover. Overhead, the warehouse roof continued to cede to the blaze, sending black smoke fuming into the air. She heard sirens in the distance. Finally, Ethan turned, his gaze locking onto Ivy with a mixture of confusion and awe. His chest heaved with each ragged breath. In that moment, the haunted expression he wore told her everything. Disbelief, gratitude, and worry.

She squeezed her eyes shut, dizzy from relief. The memory of her dream nearly suffocated her for days. Now, seeing Ethan alive and whole, she felt an odd surge of pride and guilt. She had saved him. She had changed something.

He placed a hand on her shoulder. "You... you came charging in. Did you know?"

She forced a nod, swallowing the dryness in her throat. "I felt something," she managed, wiping soot from her cheek. "I had to make sure you weren't in danger."

Ethan's eyes lingered on her with a strange softness. He glanced at Darius, who was still panting on the ground, then back at Ivy. Something unspoken passed between them. He had never believed her wholeheartedly, but he had never fully dismissed her either. They stood close in the smoky alley, the wind from the water brushing the sweat from Ivy's brow. Time seemed suspended.

Darius coughed, pulling himself to his feet. "I need to go," he said, voice shaking. "I can't be here when the fire department arrives. If they find out who I am..."

Ivy felt Ethan tense, but he nodded. "Fine. We'll be all right. Go."

Without another word, Darius hurried away, vanishing around the corner of the fence. Ethan turned back to her, eyes bright with the reflection of distant flames. She realized her mouth still tasted like ash. He watched her with undisguised concern, then laid a hand along her elbow, helping steady her.

"Are you hurt?" he asked. A line of worry deepened across his forehead. Soot smudged the bridge of his nose.

She shook her head. "I think I'm all right."

He exhaled, relief evident in his posture. A breeze ruffled his hair, carrying more sirens closer. The warehouse fire swelled behind them, groaning as beams collapsed. They both stared at the inferno, shaken.

Ethan shifted, turning to face her fully. "You saw this. Didn't you?" His voice carried a quiet certainty she had rarely heard from him.

She nodded, tears stinging her eyes. "I couldn't not come," she whispered, pressing a hand to her chest to still her galloping heart.

She could almost see the walls inside him crumbling. Skepticism, pride, and doubt all twisted together in his expression. He drew a shaky breath, looking at the raging flames, then back at her.

"Okay," he finally said, voice low and gravely serious. "Let's find out why."

CHAPTER

FOURTEEN

EMBERS AND ECHOES

The world came back in pieces, each one sharp and painful. The shriek of sirens sliced through the roar of the fire, a counter-melody of organized chaos against primal destruction. Flashing red and blue lights painted the greasy smoke and fog in frantic, strobing hues, turning the waterfront into a nightmare carnival. Ethan's lungs burned with every ragged breath, a searing reminder of the smoke that had tried to claim them. The air outside, though laced with the acrid stench of burning plastic and charred wood, was so bitingly cold it felt like a slap.

He coughed, a deep, rattling hack that tore at his throat, and bent over, bracing his hands on his knees. Soot smudged the bridge of his nose and forehead. Beside him, Ivy was doing the same, her small frame trembling, her dark curls matted with grime and sweat. He watched her wipe a hand across her cheek, leaving a dark streak on her olive skin. Her hazel-gold eyes, wide with shock, reflected the inferno of the collapsing warehouse. They were alive.

The thought was so stark, so brutally simple, that it felt like a physical blow.

Darius, a wiry man with anxious eyes whose secrets had led them here, was still panting on the ground, his face pale with terror. "I need to go," he stammered, scrambling to his feet with a panicked glance at the approaching emergency vehicles. "I can't be here when they arrive. If they find out who I am..."

Ethan felt a muscle in his jaw clench. Every journalistic instinct screamed at him to hold the man here, to get a confirmation, something more for the record. Darius was a key, a link to the hush money and the membership lists of the Seer's Circle that Lucien Grey was apparently controlling. But then he looked at Ivy, at the sheer exhaustion and fear etched onto her face, and the instinct died, replaced by something fiercer and far more protective.

"Fine. We'll be all right. Go," Ethan commanded, his voice raspy.

Darius did not need to be told twice. He scurried away, a wraith swallowed by the waterfront gloom, vanishing around a corner of the fence.

And then it was just the two of them, standing in the flaming apocalypse, the groaning death of the warehouse their only soundtrack. He watched Ivy, and the carefully constructed walls of his world crumbled into dust. He had built his life, his entire career, on a foundation of provable facts. He did not believe in anything he could not prove. He was the investigative reporter with a chip on his shoulder, the man who trusted logic.

That man was a fool. That man would be dead right now, a charred footnote in a fire report, if not for her.

"You saw this. Didn't you?" he asked, the words tasting like ash in his mouth.

She just nodded, tears finally stinging her eyes. "I couldn't not come," she whispered, her voice so fragile it nearly broke him.

Paramedics swarmed them then, brisk and professional. They smelled of antiseptic and latex, a sterile scent at odds with the grime covering him. A woman with kind eyes and a firm grip checked his pupils with a penlight, asking if he had inhaled much smoke. He answered automatically, his gaze fixed on Ivy as another paramedic wrapped a coarse orange blanket around her shoulders. She looked so small, so utterly lost in its folds.

"Sir? I need you to focus. Can you tell me your name?"

"Ethan Matson," he said, his voice distant to his own ears. He finally tore his gaze from Ivy to look at the woman. "We're fine. Just... shaken up."

A firefighter, his face grimed with soot, approached them. "You two are lucky. The whole roof gave way a minute after we got the call. Another few seconds and you'd have been trapped."

Ethan just nodded, the words lodging in his throat. He was not lucky. He had been saved. The distinction was a chasm, and he had just been thrown across it. The police were next. He saw them talking to the fire chief, their expressions grim. He knew the routine. He had been on the other side of that notepad a hundred times, asking the hard questions, looking for the angle, the lead. Now, the thought of being on the receiving end made his stomach turn.

He stepped over to Ivy's side, his hand hovering near her elbow, not quite touching. "They're going to want a statement," he said, his voice low.

She looked up at him, her wide, anxious eyes searching his. "What do we tell them?"

The question hung between them, heavy and dangerous. What could they tell them? We were meeting a secret whistleblower for a story on a psychic cult, but my friend here had a psychic premonition that the building was going to catch fire, so she showed up just in time to save us? They would be in the back of a squad car, but on their way to a psych ward, not the station. He had to concoct a lie. A lie to protect a truth that was bigger and more terrifying than any headline he had ever chased.

"Let me handle it," he said, the words feeling foreign and wrong. He was protecting a source, he told himself.

No, that was not it. He was protecting *her*. The distinction was everything.

He intercepted the officer, a young cop with a world-weary face, and launched into a carefully edited version of events. He was a reporter, he explained, meeting a confidential source about a financial scandal. He gave a deliberately vague description of Darius. He claimed the wiring had looked faulty from the moment they entered, that he had heard a pop and saw sparks just before the old insulation burst into flames. He did not mention Ivy's warning, her sudden appearance. He painted her as a colleague, someone who had accompanied him for security, someone who had been just as surprised by the fire as he was.

Each word was a betrayal of his own code, a careful step away from the man he used to be. The officer scribbled in his notepad, his expression a mixture of boredom and procedural diligence. He did not seem to question it. To him, it was just another industrial accident, another derelict warehouse going up in smoke. When the questions were done, they were told they could leave. The fire was mostly contained, though smoke still billowed into the night sky, a dark stain against the moon. He found Ivy standing by the water's edge, the blanket still around her shoulders, watching the hypnotic dance of the flames reflected on the bay's surface.

"It's over," he said softly.

She turned to him, her expression unreadable. "Is it?"

He had no answer for that. He just knew he could not leave her alone. He called Robin. He was not sure why, except that the person who was Ivy's fiercely loyal best friend felt like the right call. He needed an anchor, and he sensed Ivy did too. Robin arrived in a beat-up hatchback that rattled to a stop, their face a storm of panic and relief when they saw Ivy was safe. They flung their arms around her, holding on tight. Ethan stood back, feeling like an intruder.

"I'm taking you both home," Robin announced, their voice firm, leaving no room for argument. "My place is a mess. We'll go to Ivy's."

The drive back to the city was a blur of tense silence and streaking streetlights. Robin drove, casting worried glances at Ivy in the rearview mirror. Ivy sat huddled in the passenger seat, staring out the window, her reflection a ghostly twin superimposed over the rushing city. Ethan was in the back, the smell of smoke still clinging to his clothes, a phantom heat still radiating against his skin. He could not stop replaying it. The groaning metal. The shower of cinders raining down, separating him from Ivy. The terror of seeing her on the other side of that wall of flame, her face illuminated by the blaze, and the sheer, desperate need to get to her. He remembered how she had grabbed his wrist, her grip surprisingly strong, and pulled him toward the sliver of light from the broken loading bay door. She had not hesitated. She had run *into* the fire that he was trying to escape.

For him. The thought was a tectonic shift, rearranging everything he thought he knew about himself, about her, about the world.

Robin parked in front of Ivy's building, the one that housed her small shop, The Oracle, on the ground floor.

They killed the engine and turned, fixing Ethan with a pointed look. "You gonna be okay with her?"

"Yeah," Ethan said, his voice gravelly. "I'll make sure she's settled."

Robin nodded, their gaze softening as it rested on Ivy. "You call me if you need anything. Anything at all." They squeezed Ivy's shoulder before getting out and disappearing into a waiting rideshare they had summoned.

Now it was just them again. The silence in the car was even louder than before.

"Come on," he said gently. "Let's get you upstairs."

Ivy's apartment was a sanctuary of soft light and the lingering scent of lavender and sandalwood. It was her. It was cluttered but calm, with stacks of books, a few plush chairs, and crystals that caught the low light from a single lamp she had left on. He followed her inside, the click of the lock echoing in the quiet space. She dropped the paramedic's blanket onto a chair and stood in the middle of the room, looking lost. He saw a long, angry red scratch on her forearm where a splinter from a crate must have caught her.

"You're hurt," he said, his voice rougher than he intended.

She glanced down as if just noticing it. "It's nothing."

"It's not nothing." He went to her small bathroom, rummaging through a cabinet until he found a first-aid kit. He came back with antiseptic wipes and a bandage. She was still standing in the same spot, her arms wrapped around herself.

"Sit down, Ivy," he said, his tone softening. He gestured to the couch. She obeyed without a word, sinking into the cushions.

He knelt in front of her, the movement feeling both strange and profoundly right. He took her arm gently, his thumb brushing over her skin. It was soft, despite the grime. He cleaned the cut, his touch as careful as he could manage. She flinched when the wipe stung, a small hiss of breath escaping her lips, but she did not pull away. He was acutely aware of her stillness, of her watching him with those wide, unreadable eyes.

"I was so scared," he admitted, the confession

tumbling out before he could stop it. He kept his eyes on her arm, on the task of applying the bandage. He could not look at her face. "When the roof came down, and I couldn't see you... I thought..."

He did not finish. He did not have to.

She reached out with her other hand, her fingers tentatively touching his jaw. He froze, his own skin tingling at the contact. "Me too," she whispered.

He finally looked up. The space between them was electric, thick with unspoken words and the raw, shared memory of the fire. All the arguments, the skepticism, the tension that had defined their relationship felt like it had been burned away, leaving only this. This fragile, terrifying, and undeniable connection. He could see the faint crescent-moon birthmark behind her ear.

"Why did you do it, Ethan?" she asked, her voice barely audible. "Lie to the police?"

"Because telling the truth would have sounded insane," he said honestly. "And because they would have taken you for questioning, treated you like a suspect or a lunatic. I couldn't let that happen." He smoothed the edges of the bandage. "I couldn't protect you from the fire. I could at least protect you from that."

A single tear tracked a clean path through the soot on her cheek. He reached up and wiped it away with his thumb, his heart clenching. He wanted to pull her into his arms, to hold her until the trembling in her body stopped, to promise her that he would never let anything hurt her again. But it would be a lie. The dangers she faced were beyond his comprehension, and he knew it. All he could offer was his presence.

"I'm going to make you some tea," he said, standing up abruptly, needing to put some distance between them before he did something foolish.

He fumbled in her tiny kitchenette, finding a kettle and a box of chamomile tea. The simple, domestic act felt surreal. He, Ethan Matson, was making tea in a psychic's apartment after she had saved him from a fire she had foreseen in a vision. If he tried to write it as a scene, his editor would have laughed him out of the office.

He brought two mugs back into the living room. She had curled up on the couch, tucking her feet under her. She took the mug from him, her fingers brushing his, sending another jolt through him. They drank in silence for a long time. The city hummed outside her window, indifferent. Inside, a new world was taking shape between them.

"You believe me now," she said. It was not a question.

He let out a long, slow breath. "Yes," he said. "I'm an idiot, Ivy. I spent weeks chasing proof, demanding evidence, when the truth was standing right in front of me." The guilt was a bitter taste in his mouth.

"I'm so sorry."

"You were doing your job," she said, though her voice lacked conviction.

"No," he countered, setting his mug down with a clatter. "My job is to find the truth. I was just too blind to see what it looked like."

He looked at her, at the quiet strength in her face, the

exhaustion in her eyes. "I see you. I was wrong about everything."

She held his gaze, and for the first time, he saw the walls she kept around herself begin to lower. The anger and hurt were still there, but something else was shining through. A tentative trust.

He stayed until she finished her tea, and the tension in her shoulders seemed to ease. The exhaustion was catching up to them both, a leaden weight pulling them down.

"You should get some sleep," he said softly.

She nodded, her eyelids drooping. "You too."

He stood, hesitating at the door. "Will you be okay?"

"Robin will be here in the morning," she said. "I'll be fine."

The urge to kiss her was so overwhelming it was a physical ache in his chest. But it did not feel right. Not yet. It would feel like taking something from her, and all he wanted to do was give, his support, his belief.

"Okay," he said. "Call me. If you have another vision, if you can't sleep... if you just want to talk. Call me."

"I will," she promised.

He let himself out, closing the door softly behind him. The hallway felt cold and empty after the warmth of her apartment. He walked home through the sleeping city, the events of the night playing on a loop in his mind.

Back in his own apartment, the sterile logic of his life mocked him. The shelves of facts, the neat stacks of research. It was all a lie, a comfortable illusion he had wrapped himself in. He stripped off his smoke-infused clothes again, but this time he threw them in the trash. A symbolic, if futile, gesture. He sat at his desk and opened his notebook. He read his first entry on her.

Possibly sees things. Investigate further.

He turned to a fresh page, the pristine white a stark contrast to the chaos in his mind. He had to change his entire operational framework. He was not investigating a source. He was forming an alliance. An alliance to protect Ivy, to understand her gift, and to fight whatever was coming for them. He thought of her, and Robin, and himself. A strange, unlikely team.

He needed a name for it. Something to make it real, to define this new mission. The name of her shop came to mind, a place that had once represented everything he disdained but now felt like the center of this new reality. A faint, sheepish smile touched his lips. It was a bit pompous, but it felt right.

He wrote the words at the top of the page, pressing down hard with his pen. He circled them twice.

Project Oracle.

FIFTEEN

THE AGREEMENT

Ivy lowered herself into a metal-framed chair at an outdoor table along Valencia Street, exhaling as a cool late-afternoon breeze carried the faint scent of roasted coffee. The café's sign above them was lit in neon pink. Ethan settled in across from her. He set his leather messenger bag by his feet before opening his notebook. His gaze wandered, first to the table's wobbling edge, then drifting upward to meet her eyes. He offered her a small, warm smile, and she felt a quick shudder of relief.

Robin arrived last, armed with a lavender soda and an easy-going smirk. They sipped the purple liquid, assessing the table with a raised eyebrow before choosing a seat between Ivy and Ethan. Their presence grounded Ivy, reminding her that for the first time in weeks, she did not feel alone. For a moment, the three of them sat quietly, letting the city settle around them. A city bus hissed to a stop at the corner, and a handful of tourists snapped photos of the vibrant murals along the Mission

District's walls. On a side street, a saxophonist coaxed slow, longing notes from his instrument, weaving melody through the mild chatter of people drifting from café to café.

Ivy reached for her cup of chai tea. She found the sweetness comforting. She knew they could not ignore what was at stake. The visions, the old secrets in Cassandra's journals, the threat of more fires, there was no sense in pretending it might solve itself.

"Thanks for coming," she said quietly, letting her gaze bounce from Ethan to Robin. "I know it's been... chaotic lately."

"Chaotic is an understatement," Ethan said. Ivy noticed how he glanced at his notebook, running a pen over his lower lip, in that half-distracted motion he did while thinking. "After everything, it's clear we can't keep stumbling through this. We need a plan."

Robin tapped the rim of their glass. "Which is why we're here, yeah? Some actual ground rules before one of you decides to run into a burning building again." They cast a severe look at Ivy, though their tone remained light. "No more solo missions. No more cryptic midnight phone calls about unstoppable visions without telling the group."

Ivy smoothed the sleeve of her sweater. "I promise I won't do that again," she said. "I hate the thought of walking into danger by myself, but at the same time, I can't ignore a vision."

Ethan nodded, scribbling a note. "Then let's get into the specifics. First rule. No secrets. That includes you telling me, or Robin, or both, if you see anything. Even if you think it might be trivial."

"I can do that," Ivy agreed.

"Second," Robin said, sipping their lavender soda. "We decide as a group before you chase rumored leads or investigate random addresses. That means any tip you get, or you," they added, nodding toward Ethan, "you run it by the group. We approach it together, or we don't do it at all."

Ethan glanced at Ivy. "Works for me. If I get a new lead, I'll bring it to you first." He cleared his throat. "And probably call Robin so they can keep me from going off the deep end."

Robin grinned. "So basically, no more solo vision excursions, no more hush-hush interviews in dark alleys, and no more negotiations with shady folks behind each other's backs." They tapped the glass again, as if to emphasize each point.

Ivy took another sip of her chai, feeling an unexpected wave of relief. For so long, she had hidden her visions and her fears, partly out of shame. Sharing the burden like this was new. "I want to add something else," she murmured, catching Ethan's gaze. "Your articles. No publishing anything about me or the visions without my explicit consent. I'm not saying you can't write about what's going on, but if it puts us at risk..."

Ethan held out his palm, acknowledging her point. "I understand. I'm not here to exploit you, Ivy. I want to find the truth. But I swear, I have no intention of blasting it across headlines without your permission."

She smiled, grateful. "All right," she said, "so we have no secrets, no wandering off alone, and no publishing anything about me without my permission. It's a good start."

"Yes, it is," Ethan agreed. He jotted notes in a hasty scrawl, paused, leaning closer to the table. "One more thing. If we do come across any sign of other seers, or if your aunt reveals details about the old Circle, I'd like to know. I don't mean to pry, but I can't help unless I have the full picture."

Ivy hesitated. She knew Cassandra had been cryptic, but she also knew that secrecy had caused enough trouble. "Agreed," she said. "I don't want to keep anything from you or Robin." She ran her fingers around the rim of her cup. "She's complicated," Ivy explained. She thought of Cassandra's serious eyes, the caution in her voice whenever visions were discussed. "But she's finally helping me understand our family's legacy. She kept me in the dark for so long. I'm still sorting out how I feel about it."

Ethan looked down at his notes, as if he were memorizing every word. His voice turned gentle. "I know it's hard to trust anyone after being kept in the dark. But maybe we can build something better going forward."

Robin drummed their fingers on the table. "That means we're a team now?" A playful question hid behind their smirk, half teasing but half sincere.

Ivy exhaled slowly. "That's right. We need each other. There's too much going on for any of us to handle it alone." She paused, feeling a quiver of vulnerability. "And I guess I'm ready to share the load, for once."

A rush of relief moved through her. She watched Ethan's broad shoulders relax. She saw Robin's posture ease. For the first time, Ivy felt as though they might actually stand a chance against the unknown forces around them. Halfway through the conversation, their server arrived with fresh drinks. The aromas mingled, sweet and bitter. Around them, voices rose and fell in a symphony of casual talk.

As Ivy tasted the new chai, Ethan flipped to a fresh page in his notebook, carefully writing a header. "So, about the next steps... You said you're going to keep reading Cassandra's journals. Maybe you can teach me what to look for, so I can help decode them. The references to the older Seer's Circle are all tangled. It would help if we had more eyes on the text."

She nodded. "I know at least half a dozen passages that mention repeated patterns. If we combine that knowledge with your research skills, maybe we'll discover how the Circle functioned, and what they want now."

"And my job?" Robin asked.

Ivy tilted her head. "Your job is to keep me sane, obviously. But also, can you keep an eye on the shop while I do more research? It's too much."

Robin raised a theatrical hand. "Happily. I love bossing naive customers around. I might even read a few fortunes in your place." Their gaze turned mischievous.

Ivy laughed, a little freer than it had been in weeks. "Yes, go for it. Just remember not to promise anything you can't deliver. We have enough on our plates without a lawsuit from disappointed visitors."

Ethan gave a short chuckle, still scrawling notes. He paused. "I wanted to label all these new guidelines somehow. Like a code name."

Curious, Ivy leaned closer. "Yeah? What are you thinking?"

He cleared his throat, a slight flush coloring his ears. "I wrote down something earlier," he admitted, turning the notebook so they could see. A black-ink scrawl read, *Project Oracle?* He had circled it twice. "If that's too pompous, we can change it."

Robin snorted. "That's so dramatic, Ethan. I love it."

Ivy rolled her eyes in mock exasperation. "Project Oracle. Great. I guess that's what we're calling our little alliance."

"Well, I had to call it something," Ethan said, half defensive, half sheepish. "Can't exactly label it 'No More Crazy Solo Fire Rescues' in my notes."

Ivy reached out, letting her fingertips rest near his notebook. "It's fine. If that's what you want to call our little alliance, I'm on board," she teased. "I hope it's more than merely a fancy name for us stumbling around in the dark."

His gaze lifted to hers, something gentle in his eyes. "It is more. We might be stumbling, but you're not some story I'm going to publish. You're not simply a headline. You're..." He seemed to search for words, then settled on a quiet certainty. "You're the start of something, Ivy."

She felt a quiver run through her. The sincerity in his tone, the recognition in his expression, reached inside all the barriers she had built. Her eyes travelled from Robin's impish smile to Ethan's thoughtful gaze, and for once, she let herself be hopeful.

"Then," she said, swallowing the warmth that welled up in her chest, "let's make sure we do this right." Robin raised the lavender soda in a miniature toast. "To Project Oracle, and to not dying in any more fires." Ivy and Ethan lifted their cups, echoing the sentiment. They clinked the cups softly, a fragile pact sealed under the glow of neon lighting and city sounds.

The café's lights glinted above them, and the staff began winding down for the afternoon shift change. The city's colors outside shifted from a late golden glow to a softer lavender gloom, matching the hue of Robin's favorite drink. The breeze off the Bay grew cooler, nibbling at Ivy's cheeks.

"We should probably go soon," Ethan noted, gathering his notes and glancing at the staff who were wiping down counters inside. "Before they kick us out."

Ivy nodded, standing and slinging her bag over her shoulder. She glanced at Robin, who was cradling the near-empty soda glass. "Yeah, let's head out. Maybe we'll regroup tomorrow morning and start with the journals."

"Sounds good," Robin answered, draining the last of their drink and setting the glass down with a soft thud. "See you both tomorrow. Same place, or should we do it at the shop?"

Ivy mulled it over. "Let's do the shop. We will have the resources there, and we can spread out. And if a random customer pops in, we'll handle it."

Robin gave a mock salute. "Roger that." They gave

both Ivy and Ethan a parting look. "Cheers to the new plan."

When Robin left them to catch a rideshare, Ivy felt a wave of uncertainty. She turned to Ethan, noticing again the gold flecks in his eyes that had once made her uneasy. Now, they gave her a sense of calm. She inhaled, catching the faintest hint of coffee grounds and city fog.

He tucked his notebook under his arm. "I meant what I said. This is more than a story to me. You're more than that."

SIXTEEN

PROJECT ORACLE

A fragile truce had settled over The Oracle. It was not peace, not yet, but it was a start. The air, usually thick with the singular scent of Ivy's preferred lavender and sandalwood incense, was now a more complex blend. Ethan had brought coffee, its rich, dark aroma mingling with the sweet, herbal notes of the chamomile tea Robin was nursing. For the first time in what felt like an eternity, the small shop did not feel like a fortress or a hiding place. It felt like a headquarters.

The CLOSED sign was flipped firmly in the window, the blinds drawn low, creating a cozy, conspiratorial twilight inside. Sunlight, muted and golden, seeped through the cracks, illuminating dust motes dancing in the air like tiny, silent sprites. They had gathered around the large, circular tarot reading table, which was now covered not with cards, but with the heavy, leather-bound journals Cassandra had given Ivy. There were four of them, their covers worn smooth with time, bearing the faint, gilded imprints of crescent moons, twisting vines, and esoteric runes that seemed to shimmer in the low light.

Ivy sat between the two people in her life who had, against all odds, become her anchors. Robin, to her left, was a splash of vibrant color in the dim room. They held their mug in both hands, radiating a calm, intuitive energy that soothed the frayed edges of Ivy's nerves. To her right sat Ethan, a study in contained intensity. He had shed his journalist's armor, at least for now. Dressed in a simple, half-ironed button-down, he leaned forward, his expression a mixture of deep concentration and a newfound, cautious reverence. His leather-bound notebook lay open beside the ancient journals, a modern artifact next to relics of a forgotten world.

The weight of the moment pressed down on Ivy. This was the beginning of their pact, the first official meeting of what Ethan had semi-jokingly dubbed 'Project Oracle.' The name was a bit pompous, but it held a promise that made her feel a little less alone.

"Okay," she began, her voice a little unsteady in the quiet room. She rested her hands on the topmost journal, its leather cool and supple beneath her fingertips. "Cassandra said these belonged to my grandmother. And to her. They were trying to... map the visions. To find a pattern."

Ethan nodded, his pen poised over his notebook. "A pattern. Good. Patterns are data. Data I can work with."

Robin snorted softly into their tea. "Leave it to the

reporter to turn a century of psychic visions into a spreadsheet."

Ethan shot them a look, but it was devoid of its old skepticism. A corner of his mouth quirked up. "Hey, organization helps. If there are triggers, repeating symbols, or specific dates, we need to track them. We're looking for a system, right?"

"It's not a system, it's a language," Robin corrected gently. "And we don't have the dictionary. We have to feel it out."

Ivy watched the exchange, a faint warmth spreading in her chest. The pragmatic and the poetic, the skeptic and the believer. And she was somewhere in the middle. "You're both right," she said, deciding to be the bridge. She opened the first journal, its spine cracking softly like a breaking twig. The scent of old paper, vanilla, and something faintly metallic drifted up. The pages were a sepia-toned canvas of elegant ink.

She turned a few pages, revealing a sketch of a flock of birds spelling out a word in the sky, a vision she herself had once had. Ethan leaned closer, his shoulder brushing against hers. The contact was brief, but it sent a spark of warmth through her. "What does it say?"

"I could never make it out," Ivy admitted. "It's always too blurry, too fast."

"The word doesn't matter," Robin said, peering at the drawing. "It's the image. Birds are messengers. They travel between worlds, the sky and the earth. It's a sign that a message is trying to come through, but it's not ready to be understood yet."

Ethan scribbled a note. *Birds = undelivered message.* He looked up at Ivy. "Okay. What else did Cassandra say? About sequences?"

"She said one vision can be a trigger for another," Ivy explained, her voice gaining confidence. "They ripple outward. A symbol can appear in one person's dream, and then show up in another's reality, setting something in motion. She mentioned the red scarf from the BART accident... she showed me a sketch my grandmother had made of a man in a red scarf, decades ago."

The memory of the fire flashed in Ethan's eyes, a fleeting shadow of the terror they had shared. He cleared his throat. "Okay. So, the red scarf is a major trigger. What else?" He tapped his pen on his notebook. "We need to find the other constants."

For the next two hours, they dove into the cryptic world of Ivy's ancestors. It was slow, painstaking work. The journals were not linear diaries. They were a chaotic collage of fragmented thoughts, dream-sketches, and philosophical musings. Some pages contained meticulous charts, with arrows connecting symbols, eyes, flames, bridges, moons, in complex, star-like patterns.

Ethan, true to his word, tried to impose order on the chaos. He created a master list of recurring symbols in his notebook. The Flame. The Crescent Moon. The Bridge Crossing (and, more ominously, the Bridge Crossing Reversed). The Drowning Girl. The Man in the Coat. Each time they found one, he would note the date, if provided, and any context scribbled beside it.

"This is like trying to solve a cipher with half the key

missing," he muttered, frustration lacing his tone as he stared at a page filled with crossed-out names and heavily inked-over phrases. "They were deliberately hiding things. From whom? Each other? Or from someone else?"

"Maybe from themselves," Ivy suggested quietly. She pointed to a passage written in her grandmother's hand. "To see a path is to alter it. To record it is to make it real. Some futures are too heavy a burden to write."

Robin ran a finger over an intricate drawing of a key, its teeth fashioned from lightning bolts. "They were afraid. Can you blame them? If you saw the horrible things Ivy sees, you might want to censor yourself, too. It's a kind of psychic self-preservation."

The work was emotionally taxing. For Ivy, each page was a fresh revelation, a connection to a past she never knew she had. She saw sketches that mirrored her own childhood nightmares, felt echoes of fears that had plagued her for years. It was validating, but it was also profoundly unsettling. It was one thing to feel like an anomaly. It was another to realize she was part of a lineage defined by this beautiful, terrifying gift.

Ethan, for his part, was wrestling with his own internal shift. He approached the task with a reporter's tenacity, but the subject matter defied every rule of his profession. There were no verifiable sources here, no cross-examinable facts. There was only ink, intuition, and the undeniable evidence of the fire that still haunted his thoughts. He found himself listening intently not just to Ivy's words, but to Robin's intuitive leaps, jotting down their interpretations alongside his more structured notes.

He was learning a new kind of investigation, one that required him to trust not just what he could see, but what Ivy could *feel*.

As the afternoon wore on, a pattern began to emerge from the noise. It was faint, but it was there.

"Look at this," Ivy said. She had opened the fourth and final journal, one that seemed to belong solely to Cassandra. The handwriting was smaller, more precise, the entries more analytical than her grandmother's. Ivy pointed to a page where a complex, circular symbol was drawn with meticulous care. It looked like a stylized eye, but its iris was a labyrinth, and from its center, seven lines radiated outward, ending in seven smaller symbols. A flame, a wave, a feather, a stone, a star, a leaf, and a single, perfect drop of blood.

"I've seen this before," Ethan said instantly, flipping back through his own notes. "It's appeared three times in the other journals, but never this clearly. It's always near a mention of 'The Circle' or 'balancing the illusions.'"

Robin leaned in, their eyes narrowed in concentration. They did not touch the page, but hovered a hand over it, as if sensing its energy. "This feels... cold," they whispered. "It's powerful, but it's... controlled. Clinical. Like a machine, not a heart." They shuddered slightly. "And it feels like the ocean. Like deep, cold water."

Ivy's skin prickled. "Cassandra never explained this one to me. She just skipped past it." She stared at the symbol, a dizzying sense of vertigo washing over her. It felt ancient, significant. Beside the drawing, Cassandra had written a single, cryptic phrase.

Where the sea swallows the sky, the balance is kept.

"'Where the sea swallows the sky,'" Ethan repeated, writing it down. "A horizon line? A specific location?" He ran a hand through his hair, a gesture of deep thought. "This feels less like a vision and more like a map, or a schematic."

He pulled out his laptop, the modern device looking alien amidst the old journals. "Let's break it down. 'The Circle,' we know that's the Seer's Circle your aunt was a part of. 'Balancing the illusions'... that sounds like they were trying to control their powers, maybe prevent them from becoming overwhelming, like what happened to you at the fair."

"Or maybe they were trying to amplify them," Robin countered, their expression grim. "Power is a drug. Maybe this symbol is the key to their whole operation."

Ivy's gaze was still fixed on the intricate drawing. It seemed to pulse with a latent energy, a hum she could feel deep in her bones. "Cassandra was afraid of this page," she said with sudden certainty. "That's why she hid it from me."

Ethan's fingers flew across his keyboard. He started cross-referencing San Francisco landmarks with phrases like "coastal retreat" and "spiritual commune." He searched old newspaper archives for any mention of the Seer's Circle, however veiled. Most of it were dead ends.

"There are dozens of groups that have set up shop along the coast over the years," he said, frustrated. "Most of them fizzled out. Without a name or a more specific location, it's like looking for a needle in a haystack."

It was Robin who made the next connection. They had picked up one of the older journals again, flipping through the pages absently while Ethan typed. They stopped at a page that contained a messy, water-stained sketch of a coastline. It showed cliffs plunging into a churning sea, with a lone, gnarled cypress tree clinging to the edge.

"Ethan, look at this," Robin said, their voice sharp with excitement. They pointed to the sketch. "A gnarled cypress tree on a cliff, overlooking the ocean. That's specific."

Ethan leaned over, comparing the sketch to the satellite images on his screen. He started a new search, this time for specific coastal properties north of the city known for their unique cypress trees. Minutes ticked by in silence, the only sound the click of his keyboard and the soft rustle of journal pages.

"I've got something," he said finally, his voice low and triumphant. "There's a stretch of coastline near Muir Beach. It was once owned by a private trust in the 70s, one that funded 'alternative spiritual research.' The property was sold to a semi-private commune in the 80s. It's known for its dramatic cliffs and ancient cypress trees."

Ivy's heart hammered against her ribs. "Is the commune still there?"

"It is," Ethan confirmed, turning the laptop so they could all see. The screen showed an aerial view of a remote, windswept cliff. A small cluster of low-lying buildings was nestled into the hillside, almost invisible against the landscape. "Low-profile. They don't advertise.

It's a retreat for artists and 'spiritual seekers.' It says here they value privacy above all else."

A tidal mirror. A place where the reflection of the sky met the sea.

"That's it," Ivy breathed, a chill snaking up her spine. "That has to be the place."

"The current caretaker, the woman who runs the retreat... her name is Mirielle," Ethan said. "According to this, she was one of the original members of the trust that bought the land. She's been there for over forty years. An artist, a recluse... and according to a few old forum posts I'm finding from other psychic communities, she was rumored to be one of the most powerful seers in the Bay Area. Until she just... stopped."

The pieces fell into place, forming a picture that was both clearer and more terrifying. A hidden commune on the coast. A cryptic symbol that tied it all together.

"We have to go there," Ivy said, the words leaving her mouth before she had even consciously formed the thought. The need for answers was a physical ache, a hunger that overshadowed her fear. "We have to talk to her."

Ethan looked at her, his blue-gray eyes searching hers. He saw the determination there, the fierce resolve that had replaced her fear. He nodded slowly. "Okay," he said. "We go. But we go together. All three of us. No more solo missions." He glanced at Robin, who gave a firm, affirmative nod.

Ivy looked at the journals spread across her table, at the faces of her friends, her found family. The fear was still there, a cold knot in her stomach, but it was no longer paralyzing. It was mixed with something else now, a gleam of hope, a sense of purpose.

She had spent so much of her life feeling like she was adrift, tossed about by the chaotic waves of her visions. Now, for the first time, she felt like she was learning to navigate. She did not know what they would find at the commune, or what truths Mirielle held. But she knew she would not be facing it alone.

"Okay," she said, her voice steady and clear, echoing the quiet finality of Ethan's. "Let's go see what the sea has to say."

SEVENTEEN

THE VISIT

Ivy watched the fog roll over the winding coastal road, swallowing each curve and rocky ledge until she could only see a hazy outline of the cliffs ahead. She was in the back seat of Robin's old hatchback, her body humming with restless anticipation. The brine of the Pacific seeped through the slightly cracked windows.

Beside her, Ethan shifted, checking his phone's map. "Are you sure this is the right turn?" he asked. His voice had a quiet edge, the same subtle urgency that always crept in whenever he felt the unknown closing in.

Robin, keeping both hands on the steering wheel, let out a soft snort. "My directions are perfect," they said. They turned the car down a narrower footpath with a signpost so eroded its text was unreadable.

Ethan peered out the windshield and slid his phone into his jacket pocket. "All right. We'll see if you recognize the place in a minute or two."

Ivy settled back, letting her gaze wander. She could

feel the low buzz of the ocean echo behind her eyes, a subtle tension that set her nerves on edge. She was used to the city's clamor. Out here, the roar of waves was the only sound.

A weather-beaten cypress finally emerged from the fog, branches twisted in a shape that resembled a bent elbow. Thick knots of bark stood out against the sky. Robin slowed the hatchback and turned into a clearing. A low stone wall outlined what must be the edge of the commune's property.

They parked near a makeshift picket fence, where colored ribbons fluttered. The wind caught each strand, tangling bright greens and yellows that reminded Ivy of a half-remembered dream. She felt the pulse of the ocean far below the cliffs, rhythmic and insistent.

Ethan got out first, carefully lifting his messenger bag from the back seat. His breath misted in the cool air. "It's colder than I expected," he murmured, looking at Ivy. She smiled in reassurance, though a faint tremor coursed through her legs.

Robin hopped out next, stretching. "Fog, damp air, a hidden coastal retreat. This is exactly what I pictured," they teased. "Now all we need is someone humming folksy chants, and we have ourselves a scene from an indie film."

Ivy's lips twitched. "Don't jinx it." She zipped her canvas jacket. The scent of old sage drifted close, stirring her memory of a time when she had visited this place looking for answers that never quite arrived.

They followed a narrow footpath around three large rock formations. Wind chimes, hung from arching wooden beams, appeared in clusters. Each set tinkled with a different pitch. The entire walkway felt alive with sound, as if the air itself sang. Crystals dangled alongside them, catching stray beams of watery sunlight, casting fleeting rainbows across the moss. Surrounding everything was the crisp, mineral scent of ocean salt. Ivy felt a subtle prickle in her spine, a sign her senses recognized a place steeped in old energies.

Ahead stood a low structure of driftwood and glass, as if someone had fused a greenhouse with a cottage. Candles gleamed inside. Robin verbalised a quiet "whoa," nudging Ivy's shoulder. "This is gorgeous."

Before they reached the structure's threshold, a figure stepped out. She wore a pale shawl that wrapped around her slender shoulders, the fabric rippling like seafoam. Silver hair fell in two thin braids, framing a face etched with lines of weariness. Her eyes were hollow, as though they had seen too many storms. Ivy's pulse jumped in recognition.

Mirielle. The former seer Ivy had only heard whispers about, rumored to have retreated from everything. She swallowed, goosebumps rising on her arms.

"Welcome," Mirielle said. Her voice was low, a near-croon that nevertheless carried. She glanced at Ethan and Robin, then focused on Ivy. "I wondered when your steps would lead you back, child."

Ivy stepped forward. "Thank you for letting us come." She hesitated, searching for something more personal to say.

Mirielle's expression shadowed. "I never forget the

ones who carry the sight. And you, dear one, bring it everywhere you go." She turned slightly, gesturing for them to follow her inside.

They obeyed, stepping over a threshold set with smooth, sea-worn stones. The space was comfortable, although nearly barren. A low table stood in the center, draped in a cloth embroidered with geometric symbols. Shelves along one wall held chipped mugs and jars stuffed with dried plants. Crystals hung from the beams overhead, reflecting tiny spots of light across the wooden floor. Robin found a stool beside a stack of folded blankets. Ethan lingered near Ivy, scanning every corner.

Mirielle moved to a narrow table at the back and picked up a smooth kettle. Curving vines were carved along its side. She poured hot water into small cups, steam curling in delicate shapes. The earthy smell of nettle leaves soon followed. She offered each of them a cup. Ivy accepted hers, cradling the heat between her palms. The rising steam coated her face with gentle warmth. Robin gave a grateful nod, while Ethan murmured a quiet thanks. Mirielle's gaze shot back to Ivy.

"Some gifts come with a timer," the older woman said, voice barely above a whisper. "The mind either opens wider... or breaks. You should know how close you stand to that line."

The blunt words made Ivy's stomach tighten. "What do you mean?" She felt Ethan shift closer. He did not speak, but his presence steadied her.

Mirielle took a sip of her own tea, eyes hooded. "I knew you were coming because the sea told me. Or perhaps my own leftover gift did. Either way, you stand on a threshold where your power is forcing itself out. Until you learn what it demands, it will press you harder." She set her cup on the table. "Some do not survive that strain."

Robin sat very still. Ethan, too, kept his silence, though Ivy sensed the ripple of tension in his shoulders. She inhaled slowly, her pulse hammering in her ears. She wondered if Mirielle sensed the warehouse incident or the daily weight that Ivy felt simmering in her chest.

"I've had visions my whole life," Ivy said. "I struggle with them more now that... events have changed." She chose her words carefully. "I'm trying to learn control. But you seem to think I'm already at risk of losing that."

Mirielle's hollow eyes softened. "Child, you're only at risk if you choose ignorance. The right knowledge is always within your reach. The question is whether it sets you free or chains you deeper."

Ivy set her untouched tea down. Unease circled in her chest. She recalled standing here as a teenager, searching for a cure to nightmares. Perhaps the woman had always known the path Ivy would walk.

Robin cleared their throat. "You said you used to be a seer. Are you not one now?"

A faint curve danced at the corners of Mirielle's mouth. "That part of me is dormant. I locked it away after it threatened to overtake my sanity. The cost of shutting it out was high." She turned her gaze to Ivy as if to impart that the same choice might lie ahead.

Ethan lifted his tea, taking a careful sip. His eyes

shifted to Mirielle. "Is there anything you can teach Ivy? Something that might help her manage these... visions?"

Mirielle inclined her head. The wind outside rattled the chimes, sending a wave of soft music through the open walls. "Courses of action exist, but I sense that Ivy must chart them herself. Others can guide, but no one can carry the load for her."

Ivy tried not to flinch at the finality in Mirielle's tone. The words were reminiscent of every uneasy moment she had endured, alone. She had been hoping for a map, a method that would make the next steps clear.

Mirielle poured more hot water into her cup. The steam rose again, spiralling around them. "Stay the night here if you'd like. We have a guest lean-to near the orchard. It's quiet. Calming, too." Her stare settled on Ivy's face. "I doubt your dreams will remain calm, though. Your power stirs the tides themselves."

Ivy's heartbeat thudded. "We appreciate it," she said softly, glancing at Ethan and Robin. Robin gave a small nod, eyes bright with curiosity. Ethan pressed his lips into a thoughtful line and nodded. The drive back in the dark fog did not seem appealing, and they had come this far seeking real answers.

Mirielle offered a gentle smile. "Finish your tea, walk the property if you wish. Then rest. I will send someone to show you the lean-to when you are ready. At dawn, I can share a few protective techniques and an herbal mixture. It might help you find yourself in your visions."

Ivy managed a cautious smile in return. "Thank you," she breathed, feeling a lump of relief lodge in her throat.

They spent the next hour exploring the commune's grounds. Wooden posts ringed the edges of a garden patch full of herbs that looked half-wild. Wind chimes persisted everywhere. Ethan took note of how neatly the place was arranged. Robin wandered with open fascination, occasionally crouching to examine a quirky arrangement of crystal shards or sniff a cluster of dried sage bundle near a row of potted plants. Eventually, a slender woman approached, offering them lanterns and leading them along a winding path to a small lean-to shelter perched against a stand of gnarled trees. A wide porch stretched out over the slope, offering a staggering view of the ocean. Ivy peered across the misty distance. The waves heaved in rhythmic arcs, as though breathing with some ancient life.

Sunset arrived in muted layers of violet and orange. They built a small fire in a circle of stones, warming their hands while the ocean wind ruffled their hair. Robin teased Ethan about the first time he had tried herbal teas, earning a smirk from him. Ivy felt a fleeting sense of normalcy.

When the wind picked up, they doused the fire and moved inside. The lean-to had three cots lined with thin quilts. Sleep called to her, though her mind chased worries in circles. She crawled onto a cot, tucking her jacket over her legs. Ethan settled on the adjacent cot, quietly checking on her. He placed a hand over hers, gently squeezing. Robin yawned and flopped onto the third cot.

Eventually, they drifted into silence, lulled by the sound of waves colliding with the rocky shore. The chimes outside blended with the distant rush, forming a lullaby that coaxed Ivy's eyes shut. She glimpsed Ethan's silhouette in the darkness and felt a gradual calm.

She sank, and the dream came.

The cliffs dissolved into an infinite stretch of rolling water. Moonlight cast a pale glow that turned the ocean's surface to silver. Ivy stood barefoot on the shore and strode forward. With each step, the water receded until it transformed beneath her feet, shifting and clarifying into a layer of solid glass. It was as if she stood on a gleaming mirror that extended to the horizon. Her breath caught as she saw, faintly, something moving below that transparent surface. Dark shapes stirred in the depths, gliding with silent purpose.

CHAPTER

EIGHTEEN

THE TIDAL MIRROR

Dawn at the edge of the continent was not a gentle affair. It was a raw, elemental birth. A thick blanket of fog, glowing with a soft, pre-dawn luminescence, clung to the cliffs, so dense that the world seemed to end just a few feet from where they stood. The air was cold and wet, saturated with the smell of salt, damp earth, and the faint, clean scent of blooming sea thrift. The only sounds were the eternal, rhythmic crash of the waves far below, a deep, resonant heartbeat, and the chaotic, tinkling music of a hundred wind chimes stirred by the restless Pacific breeze.

Ivy stood on a flat, rocky promontory overlooking the churning white void. Her arms were wrapped tight around her middle, a futile attempt to ward off a chill that felt like it was seeping up from the stone itself. A few paces behind her, Ethan and Robin stood as silent witnesses, their forms muted silhouettes against the growing light. Ethan's posture was rigid, a statue of coiled concern. Robin, ever the anchor, simply watched her, their presence a quiet, unwavering statement of support.

Mirielle stood beside Ivy, her slender frame seemingly impervious to the cold. She wore the same pale shawl as the day before, its fabric rippling like seafoam in the wind. Her silver hair was unbound today, a wild mane that danced around a face etched with the wisdom of a thousand storms. She had not spoken since leading them here, simply waiting, her gaze fixed on the place where the sea and sky were supposed to meet.

"The gift is an ocean," Mirielle said at last, her voice a low croon that was nearly carried away by the wind. "Inside you. Most seers spend their lives tossed about in a small boat, at the mercy of every tide, every squall. They believe the goal is to calm the storm. They are wrong. You cannot calm an ocean."

She turned her hollow, ancient eyes to Ivy. "The goal is to find your anchor."

This was to be her training. Not a lecture or a lesson, but a metaphor brought to life. Ivy swallowed, her throat dry. "How?"

"By remembering you are not the water. You are the shore," Mirielle said. "The waves of vision will crash against you, always. They will erode you, change you, pull at your foundations. But you must remain. You must learn to feel the pull of the tide without letting it drag you out to sea."

She gestured for Ivy to close her eyes. "Listen. Not with your ears. Feel the world around you. Find one thing that is undeniably real, something that belongs only to you, here and now. Let that be your anchor."

Ivy obeyed, shutting her eyes against the whiteness. At first, all she could feel was the chaos. The roar of the waves was a physical pressure against her eardrums. The wind was a thousand icy needles on her skin. The tinkling of the chimes was a dizzying, discordant symphony. And beneath it all, the thrum of psychic energy from this place, a powerful, ancient current, threatened to pull her under. Images flashed at the edges of her consciousness. The fiery collapse of the warehouse, the vacant, milky eyes of the man in the park, the mocking smile of Lucien Grey from her childhood drawing.

Panic coiled in her stomach. I'm going to lose it, she thought. Just like at the fair.

"No," Mirielle's voice cut through the noise, calm and clear. "You are the shore, Ivy Lewis. The vision is the wave. Let it crash, but do not let it take you. Find your anchor. Now."

Ivy desperately searched for something to hold onto. The feeling of the rough, cold stone beneath the thin soles of her boots. The taste of salt on her lips. The ache in her shoulders from sleeping on the cot. Nothing was strong enough. The psychic tide was pulling her out, the images growing sharper, more insistent. She felt a familiar, terrifying dizziness, the world tilting.

Then, she found it.

Her own heartbeat.

It was frantic, a panicked bird beating against the cage of her ribs. But it was hers. Steady. Rhythmic. Thump-

thump. Thump-thump. It was the one sound that was not the ocean, not the wind, not the visions. It was the engine of her own life.

She focused on it with ferocious intensity. *I am here,* she thought, syncing her breath to the rhythm. *This body is mine. This heartbeat is mine.*

She felt a wave of images crest, a marble corridor, a man in a violet coat, but instead of being consumed by it, she felt it break against the solid shore of her own pulse. The vision was still there, a powerful, roaring presence, but it was *outside* of her, no longer a part of her. She could observe it without drowning in it. For the first time, there was a space, however small, between Ivy the woman and the visions that haunted her.

She let out a shaky breath and opened her eyes. The fog had begun to thin, and a sliver of brilliant, molten gold appeared on the horizon. The world felt sharper, the colors more vibrant. The training had lasted only minutes, but she felt as drained as if she had run a marathon.

"Good," Mirielle said, a rare, faint smile touching her lips. "The anchor held."

Ivy looked back at her friends. Ethan's shoulders had relaxed, and he gave her a small, relieved nod, his eyes full of a warmth that made her heart skip. Robin offered a wide, proud grin. The relief of not being alone in this was so potent it almost brought her to her knees.

"That..." Ivy started, her voice hoarse. "That was the hardest thing I've ever done."

"It will get easier," Mirielle promised. "And it will get harder. Your power is surging, child. The veils are tearing.

You must practice this every day. Find your anchor, or the ocean inside will claim you for its own."

She led them back from the cliff's edge, along a winding path of sea-worn stones. The rising sun had finally broken through, casting long, dramatic shadows across the commune. The sheer, raw beauty of the place was staggering. It felt timeless, a pocket of the world immune to the frantic pace of the city she had left behind.

As they approached Mirielle's driftwood-and-glass cottage, Ivy's gaze fell upon a small, secluded corner of the garden she had not noticed before. There, nestled amongst a riot of wild lavender and sage, was a bench made from a single, massive piece of gnarled driftwood, bleached nearly white by sun and salt. Beside it sat a circle of smooth, gray stones, arranged in a pattern that was both random and intentional.

The moment she saw it, a dizzying wave of déjà vu washed over her, so powerful it buckled her knees. It was not a vision. It was a memory. A memory that felt ancient, buried under layers of silt and time. The scent of lavender, the specific curve of the driftwood bench, the precise arrangement of the stones, her senses screamed with a familiarity that her conscious mind could not place.

"Ivy?" Ethan was at her side in an instant, his hand on her elbow, steadying her. "What is it? What do you see?"

"I... I don't know," she stammered, pressing a hand to her forehead. "I've been here before. Right here. At this bench."

Mirielle, who had been walking ahead, stopped and turned. She looked at Ivy, then at the driftwood bench, and a profound, weary sadness filled her eyes. "Ah," she said softly, as if a long-expected guest had finally arrived. "So, the remembering begins."

She waited for Ivy to regain her footing before speaking again, her voice gentle. "Yes, child. You have been here before."

Ivy stared at her, her mind struggling to connect the pieces. "What? I would have remembered this place."

"Would you?" Mirielle countered, her gaze holding Ivy's. "You were only five years old. And your parents did not bring you here for a holiday. They brought you here for a cure."

The words landed like stones in the quiet morning air. A cure. Ivy's thoughts flew to her mother, Anna, the cognitive neuroscientist who dismissed anything that could not be measured or proven. The woman who had dismissed Ivy's childhood predictions, desperate for her daughter to be normal. The idea that the same woman would bring her tormented child to a psychic retreat on a remote cliffside was so contradictory, so utterly unbelievable, that Ivy almost laughed. But the aching familiarity of the driftwood bench told her it was true.

"My mother?" Ivy whispered, the name tasting like a betrayal on her tongue. "She brought me *here*?"

Ethan's grip on her elbow tightened, his anger a silent, radiating heat. Robin stepped closer to Ivy's other side, their face a mask of shocked disbelief.

"She was desperate," Mirielle said, her tone devoid of judgment. "And you were a tormented child. You didn't just have nightmares, Ivy. You lived in them. You would wake screaming about fires and floods, about faces you couldn't have known, about tragedies that had not yet come to pass." She gestured toward the cottage. "Come. There is tea. And a story you are now old enough to hear."

Inside the spartan cottage, the air was warm and smelled of the nettle tea Mirielle had served them before. They sat on woven cushions around the low table, a tense silence hanging between them. Mirielle poured the steaming, earthy liquid into four chipped ceramic cups, her movements slow and deliberate.

"Your mother found me through a colleague," Mirielle began, cradling her cup in her gnarled hands. "A psychologist, of all things. One who had quietly referred other... unique cases to me over the years. When Anna arrived with you and your father, she was at her breaking point. She was a woman of science, confronted with something that defied every law she held sacred. And she was terrified. Not just for you, but *of* you."

Ivy flinched, the words a confirmation of a fear she had long held. Her mother had not just been dismissive. She had been afraid of her own daughter.

"You were drawing things," Mirielle continued, her gaze drifting to a point somewhere over Ivy's shoulder. "Endlessly. Pictures of a man with platinum hair and cruel eyes. Sketches of a circle of people standing around a fire. You were too young to explain what you saw, but the images poured out of you. Your mother believed you were schizophrenic, that you were having dangerous hallucinations. Your father... he was more open-minded, but he was lost, caught between his wife's clinical fear and his daughter's inexplicable terror."

"They asked me to stop it," Mirielle said, her voice heavy with regret. "To sever your connection to... whatever you were seeing. To make you normal."

"And you did?" Ivy's voice trembled, a mixture of accusation and heartbreak.

"No," Mirielle said firmly, her hollow eyes meeting Ivy's. "I would never sever a seer from her gift. To do so is a violence that can shatter the soul. It is what happened to me, long ago." She took a shaky breath. "But I could see the state you were in. The visions were too strong for a child's mind to bear. You had no anchor, no shore. The ocean was drowning you. So, I offered them a different solution. Not a cure. A veil."

"A veil?" Ethan asked, his voice tight with suspicion.

"A form of psychic protection," Mirielle explained. "I guided Ivy through a series of deep meditations, right there, on that driftwood bench. I did not block her gift. Instead, I helped her build walls around the memories. I helped her mind create a veil between her conscious self and the visions that were traumatizing her.

It was meant to be a temporary shield, a way to quiet the waters until she was old enough to learn control, to build her own anchor."

She looked directly at Ivy, her expression filled with a deep, profound sorrow. "I instructed your parents to bring you back when you were a teenager. I told them that the veils would begin to thin as your power grew with age, and that you would need guidance to navigate the remembering. I warned them that treating the quiet as a cure would be dangerous."

A heavy, sickening silence filled the cottage. The implications of Mirielle's words crashed down on Ivy with the force of a physical blow. Her mother had conspired to have Ivy's own memories, her own childhood, hidden from her. She had taken the temporary silence Mirielle had offered and willfully, desperately, treated it as a permanent cure. She had never brought Ivy back. She had chosen denial over guidance, a lie over the truth.

"She... she let me believe I was broken," Ivy whispered, the words scraping her raw throat. All the years of self-doubt, the psychology degrees she pursued to try and explain away her own mind, the shame she felt with every intuitive flash, it was all a lie constructed by her mother's fear. "She chose to let me forget."

"The energy of a strong vision, especially a traumatic one, never truly disappears," Mirielle said softly. "It leaves an echo, a residue. But the past does not stay buried, child. And the power inside you is too strong. It has been pushing against those walls for years. Now, they are beginning to tear. That is why your visions have returned with such chaotic, overwhelming force. You are not just learning to see. You are remembering a language you were forced to forget."

Ethan finally spoke, his voice a low growl of protective fury. "You're saying her mother knowingly subjected her to this? Left her completely unprepared for what was coming?"

"I am saying," Mirielle corrected, her gaze unwavering,

"that a frightened woman made a choice she believed was right, and that choice has had profound consequences. The love of a parent can be a powerful shield, but it can also be a gilded cage."

The truth of it settled on Ivy's shoulders, a crushing weight. She thought of her mother's sharp, professional demeanor, her tidy neutral clothes, her desperate need for a rational, explainable world. And she understood. Anna Lewis had not been cruel. She had been terrified. She had seen an ocean raging inside her daughter and, instead of teaching her to swim, had tried to pretend the water was not there.

Ivy stood up, the cushion falling to the floor behind her. She walked to the open doorway of the cottage, staring out at the cliffside, at the driftwood bench. The memories were still gone, locked behind a veil she did not know how to part, but the *feeling* of them was there, a phantom limb, an ache for a part of herself that had been amputated.

She felt Ethan come to stand beside her. He did not touch her, but his presence was a solid, reassuring warmth against the cold sea air.

"What now?" she asked, her voice directed at the vast, indifferent ocean. "How do I tear down a wall I don't remember building?"

"You don't tear it down," Mirielle's voice came from behind them. "You let it dissolve. You practice anchoring. You allow the memories to surface as they will. But you must be prepared. The process will be painful. And it will make you a beacon."

Ivy turned. "A beacon?"

"The tearing of a veil releases a tremendous amount of psychic energy," Mirielle said, her expression grim. "Think of it as a lighthouse, suddenly relit in a storm. It will attract attention. From all corners of this city's hidden world. Others with the sight, those who are sensitive to such currents, will feel it. They will be drawn to you."

She took a step closer, her eyes boring into Ivy's. "Some will come to help. Others... others will be drawn to your light like moths to a flame, seeking to control it, or to extinguish it altogether."

Her words hung in the air, a chilling prophecy that resonated with the fear Ivy had felt since this all began. The man with milky-white eyes in the park. The cryptic letter. They were not just happening *to* her. They were *responding* to her. To the awakening happening inside her.

"Be wary of those who are drawn to you from the shadows," Mirielle warned, her voice dropping to a whisper. "A bright light can be a guide, but it also reveals one's position to those who hunt in the dark."

They left the commune an hour later, after Mirielle had given Ivy a small pouch of dried herbs, yarrow for courage, mugwort for psychic clarity, and lavender for calm, and a final, solemn nod. The drive back was heavy with a new kind of silence. The shock had settled into a deep, foundational ache inside Ivy. Robin tried to fill the space with quiet, comforting chatter, but eventually, they too fell silent, sensing that Ivy needed to be alone with the ruins of her own history.

Ethan sat beside her in the back of the rattling hatchback, his presence a silent promise. He did not offer platitudes or easy solutions. He simply sat with her in her grief and confusion, and for that, she was profoundly grateful.

She stared out the window as the wild, rugged coastline gave way to the familiar, fog-draped streets of San Francisco. She felt like she was returning from a foreign country, a stranger in her own home, in her own mind. Her childhood was not what she thought it was. Her mother's love was a story far more complicated than she had ever imagined. And her own gift, the ocean inside her, was threatening to pull her under just as its waves were beginning to reveal the forgotten things hidden in their depths.

Mirielle's final warning echoed in her mind. *You will be a beacon.* She did not feel like a beacon. She felt like a girl standing on a cliff in the fog, listening to the roar of an approaching storm, and hoping her anchor would be strong enough to hold.

NINETEEN

THE WARNING

Moonlight stretched across a corridor of polished marble, its silvery glow cutting a path over black tile. Ivy stood at the center of that hall, feeling the chill of stone beneath her bare feet. She could not remember how she had arrived. No windows lined these walls, yet white moonlight poured in as though invited, weaving over the floor in slanted bands. The air smelled faintly of damp stone and something harder to place, like a long-burned candle.

She took a hesitant step. With each footfall, her pulse intensified. The walls were blank except for occasional arches that hinted at hidden passages. She wondered if someone watched her from beyond those curves. Movement drew her attention. From the darkest corner of the corridor, a figure emerged. He wore a fitted coat the color of twilight violets. His footsteps made no echo, as if the marble did not dare announce his presence. He stepped closer, his face obscured in the gloom until moonlight brushed the edges of his features. The shape of his hair, the angle of his jaw, both seemed strangely familiar, yet she could not recall where she had seen him before.

"You think you're the only one dreaming?" he asked, voice quiet but resonant. The question curled around her with a gentle intrusion.

She pressed her back against the cool marble. "I don't know what you mean."

He stopped mere steps away, a silhouette carved by moonlight. "I do," he replied, smoothing a hand over the front of his elegant coat. His eyes never wavered from hers. "You're the message, but you may not be the messenger."

Time hovered, and the corridor lengthened in both directions, as though the space was stretching around them. The man melted deeper into shadow. Her chest tightened with unspoken questions. A blink later, she was alone again. The corridor's edges shimmered. She braced a hand on the marble, breathing fast. The moonlight seemed to pulse along with her heartbeat. Then the world jolted. She fell backward. A rush of cold air blasted across her face. The marble corridor disintegrated like an old painting. Darkness swallowed everything.

Ivy jerked awake, her sheets damp with sweat. She lay in bed, panting. It took several seconds for her eyes to adjust to the faint glow of a lamp she had forgotten to switch off. Her heart still hammered. She pressed a trembling hand to her mouth and breathed in a shaky gulp of air. She glanced at her phone on the nightstand. The screen read a time far too early, just past four in the morning. Outside, fog pressed against the glass, and beyond it, San Francisco embraced the dark. She forced herself to lie back, though she doubted sleep would return. Her mind reeling, she tried to recall each detail. The marble floor, the violet coat, and the man's voice that seemed both soothing and ominous. His words would not let go.

When dawn finally came, she overheard faint clinking from the next room of the apartment. Ethan's steady presence filtered through the closed door. The smell of coffee drifted under the gap. She stretched, feeling the sticky remnants of sweat on her skin. As soon as she stood, the subtle ache in her legs reminded her of how tense she had been. She quickly splashed water on her face in the bathroom, noticing her reflection seemed a little paler. She hurried to dress, slipping on a soft sweater and a comfortable pair of jeans. The mirror reflected her face, showing circles under her eyes. The dream remained vivid, lodged in her chest.

In the kitchen, she found Ethan standing near the sink with two mugs on the counter. A fresh pot of coffee steamed beside him. He was alert, hair still rumpled, dressed in a plain gray T-shirt and jeans. His gaze lifted as she entered.

"You're up earlier than usual," he observed, pushing one mug toward her. She offered a tight smile, reaching for the coffee to give her hands something to do. Even the warmth of the ceramic against her palms did not dispel the chilly feeling clinging to her core.

"I had trouble sleeping," she admitted. She took a sip and felt the hot liquid slip down her throat, stoking a small surge of energy. "Thought I might as well start the day."

Ethan studied her carefully. "Rough night?" His voice carried gentle concern, but she heard the sharp intelligence behind it.

She swallowed. Her mouth felt strangely dry. "Just restless. I guess I couldn't turn my mind off."

His stare lingered a moment longer, and she could practically feel the weight of his concern. "Are you sure?" he asked, placing his mug down. She noticed his notepad half-buried under the morning newspaper. Their new vow was to keep no secrets. Her stomach tightened.

She inhaled. "I had another dream. Different from the ones on the coast, but still unsettling."

Ethan's stance shifted, relief and concern merging across his face. "Tell me."

"I was standing in this huge space. Marble floors, midnight sky overhead, the moon shining through some unseen window. A man stood there, wearing a dark purple coat. He spoke to me, said something about me being the message but not the messenger." Her brow creased. "It felt personal, like he knew me."

Ethan extended a hand, resting it gently on her forearm. "What did his face look like?"

She shook her head. "Vague. He was tall, confident, but the shadows kept half his face hidden. His voice was... strangely soft, and it was almost like I recognized it. I can't figure out who he is."

He exhaled softly, eyes moving to the notepad. "It could be someone we've come across. Or it might be something deeper, like your mind warning you," he said, sounding uncertain.

Ivy clutched her mug. "The strangest part was how real it felt. It wasn't a typical nightmare with the usual chaos. Everything was sharp and quiet, like a staged performance." She paused, biting her lower lip. "But I was terrified. And I'm not sure why. He didn't threaten me. He... made me feel that I'm part of something bigger that I still don't understand."

Ethan's gaze softened, his thumb brushing against the back of her hand where it rested on the table. "I know. But every new piece of this puzzle, even the frightening ones, gets us closer to the truth." He took a final sip of his coffee and glanced at his watch, his expression shifting from concern to determination. "Look, I have to run. I have a lead I need to follow up on at the newsroom."

Ivy's stomach tightened slightly at the familiar, driven look in his eyes, the one that had once been aimed squarely at her. "A lead? On this?"

"On everything," he said, his vagueness a gentle dismissal. He stood, dropping a few bills on the table. "I'll call you later. If you see anything else, even a flash, you text me. No secrets, remember?" He leaned down, his voice dropping lower. "We'll figure this out, Ivy. I promise." He gave her hand one last, reassuring squeeze before turning and disappearing into the lunchtime crowd, leaving her alone with the dregs of her tea and the lingering chill of the vision.

The hours that followed were a torment of restless energy. Ivy tried to lose herself in the familiar routines of her shop, but the quiet scent of lavender and sandalwood offered no comfort. The man in the violet coat haunted her thoughts, his words echoing with a significance she could not grasp. *You're the message.* This felt different from the other visions, less like a warning of external danger and more like a key to an internal lock. A lock she was convinced Cassandra not only knew about but had perhaps even helped install. Waiting for Ethan's call suddenly felt unbearable. She could not sit by while he chased down his leads. This was her history. She needed answers, and she knew the only person who held them was her aunt.

Driven by a new, sharp-edged resolve, she closed the shop early. The late-afternoon fog was already rolling in as she made her way to Cassandra's townhouse, the chill in the air mirroring the dread coiling in her gut. She climbed the front steps, her heart pounding a nervous rhythm against her ribs. As her hand reached for the door, she froze, the sound of raised, angry voices from within slicing through the quiet street. One was her aunt's, sharp and cold. The other, to her shock and dismay, was Ethan's.

Ivy climbed the front steps of Cassandra's townhouse with reluctance knotting her stomach. The late-afternoon fog brushed her cheeks, and her breath came out in small, clouded puffs. She squinted at the imposing door. A faint glow seeped through the tall windows to her right. She sensed a confrontation crackling inside. She heard muffled voices as she placed her palm against the door. She recognized the deeper timbre of Ethan's voice. There was a distinct note of anger in it that made her spine stiffen.

Cassandra's tone followed, equally curt. She tried the knob, surprised to find it unlocked, and slipped into the dim foyer. The old house smelled of incense and old memories. Fading light from the narrow hallway lamp illuminated a shelf of antique books, half of them turned sideways and dusty. An old mirror hung nearby, draped in gauzy cloth, so only its edges peeked out. Ivy stepped forward. The conversation was clearer now.

"You never mentioned this," Ethan said. His frustration echoed off the walls. "I found an archived article. It says 'Local Seer Dies in Ritual Gone Wrong. Witness Uncooperative.' The witness was you, Cassandra."

Ivy froze. She felt the weight of his accusation deepen the air. She moved closer, passing through the arched entry into the main sitting room. Cassandra's silhouette came into view. She leaned against a tall chair, posture taut. Ethan stood several paces away, an old newspaper clipping in his hand.

Cassandra's eyes were cold. "Would it have mattered?" she said in a low voice. "You were never here for her, only for the story."

Ivy's heart lurched. She cleared her throat softly. The reflection of the little lamp gleamed against a row of crystals on a small table near the wall. She saw Ethan's shoulders tense at Cassandra's words. For a moment, he looked as if he wanted to argue, but his awareness told him they were no longer alone. He turned toward the doorway. His face held a trace of guilt when he caught sight of Ivy.

"Ivy," Ethan managed, voice barely above a whisper. "I didn't expect you so soon."

She went inside fully, her gaze darting between her aunt and Ethan. Cassandra folded her arms, her expression shuttered. She swallowed and moved forward, noticing that he still gripped a corner of the article as though it might slip away. A quick glance revealed the headline, *Local Seer Dies in Ritual Gone Wrong.*

"I heard enough," Ivy said, voice trembling. "You've been digging into her past, Ethan?" Her hazel eyes darted from him to Cassandra. "And you," she added, her glare shifting to her aunt, "you never said anything about a seer dying."

Cassandra's thin braids drifted against her shoulders as she turned sharply, exhaling. There was a sorrow behind her guarded stare, but her tone remained brisk. "There are many events I have not told you about, child. Believe me when I say it was for a reason."

Ivy's pulse pounded. She looked at Ethan. "I discovered it by accident," he said. "I've been searching for leads, trying to connect the patterns in your family history. I found references to a secret society of seers." He gestured to the article. "This jumped out at me. I recognized Cassandra's name, so I followed the lead. I wanted to know if seeing that old tragedy might help us understand what we're dealing with."

Cassandra cut back in. "And by doing so, you have pried open wounds that were better left to rest. I cooperated however I could. The officials wrote it as a 'ritual gone wrong' to explain away something they could not understand."

Ivy frowned. Her chest felt heavy. "So, a seer died during some... ritual? And you were the only witness?"

Cassandra released a soft, mirthless laugh. "If you think the city's official records ever captured the truth, you are mistaken. The death was not so simple. It shrouded us all in regret."

Ethan watched Cassandra with barely contained frustration. He rubbed the back of his neck, as though uncertain how to proceed. "Look," he replied quietly, "I wasn't trying to exploit this. I..."

"Of course you were," Cassandra snapped. "You are a reporter who thrives on unearthing secrets. I know your kind, Ethan Matson. And I see how you look at Ivy. You are torn between caring for her and wanting to claim her story as your trophy."

Each word struck like a lash. Ivy inhaled sharply, trying to quell her stomach. She glanced down at the old clipping in Ethan's hand. The house felt too small, the air too charged.

Ivy felt her throat tighten. She glanced up at him, seeing the regret in his eyes. She spoke in a thin voice. "I trusted you, Ethan. I thought we agreed, no secrets, no digging behind each other's backs." Warm tears pricked the corners of her eyes, but she refused to let them fall. "Why didn't you tell me you found this article?"

He opened his mouth, but only silence came out. Finally he pressed his lips into a line. "I wanted tangible proof. I wanted to do more research before I worried you. I thought if I could piece everything together and protect you from half-truths, that would be better."

The explanation tasted hollow. "You thought you were protecting me? Maybe you were protecting yourself. If you had told me sooner, I could have helped. But instead, you've turned this into your personal investigation."

Cassandra's gaze darted between them, though her expression remained pinched. "He does not understand, Ivy. He never did. You fought so hard to prove yourself to him and now look at where it has left you."

Ivy turned to Cassandra, the knot of betrayal shifting targets. "You speak like you have all the answers, yet you hide things at every turn. You keep speaking in riddles. Did you plan to keep this a secret forever?" She gestured at the clipping. "A seer died, you were there, and you did not think it was relevant?"

Cassandra's jaw tightened. "It was not my story to share. I only bore witness and have no interest in tarnishing the memory of a friend who died in confusion and agony. I told you, child, many aspects of the old ways are best left forgotten."

"But they are not forgotten." Ivy's voice cracked. "They haunt us no matter what. You taught me that visions don't vanish because we pretend they do." She drew a shaky breath. "I needed you to be honest, to guide me, not to hide more secrets until Ethan dug them up."

Something like pain flashed in Cassandra's eyes. "I believed the darkness of that night would only pull you deeper into harm. You are not prepared for every truth."

An old floorboard creaked beneath Ivy's foot as she shifted her weight. She took in Ethan's clenched fists, Cassandra's sharp posture, and the faint smell of burnt sage lingering near a candle on a corner table. She felt suffocated.

Ethan exhaled, desperate. "I did not do this for a headline. I was..." He paused, meeting her gaze. "I was afraid that if I told you before I had more evidence, you would leap headlong into danger. I tried to hold it close, at least until the pieces formed a coherent story. I did not want to see you hurt."

"Yet you went behind my back and called Cassandra without telling me," Ivy said. "You confronted her, cornered her. I feel like I walked into a war zone I should have known about. I despise being left out like a would-be victim you both need to shield."

Cassandra laid a hand on the chair's back. "Ivy, I never wanted you to see that article. I am sorry you had to learn of it this way."

Ivy stared at her aunt's face, searching for sincerity but seeing only guilt laced with resignation. A heavy sadness filled her chest. "And you, Cassandra, I needed you. You knew I was seeking answers, and yet you stayed silent on something so major. That is betrayal too."

A faint tremor moved through Cassandra's shoulders, as though she wanted to speak but chose not to. Ivy heard the faint ticking of a clock somewhere deeper in the townhouse. She had the disorienting sense that time itself had stopped here, trapping them in this painful moment. An uncomfortable lull settled.

She swallowed hard. Her voice grew stronger. "I trusted you," she repeated, focusing on Ethan, though her words carried the weight of her accusation for both of them. Her chest felt tight, tears burning behind her eyes. She turned to Cassandra, voice taking on a tremor. "And I needed you."

Ethan moved closer, lifting a hand as if to reach for her, but she sidestepped him. She refused to meet his gaze again, certain she would break down if she saw the regret in his eyes.

"Ivy," he said softly. "Please let me explain…"

"You already did," she whispered, cutting him off. "And so did Cassandra. I do not want to hear another half-baked explanation. This is my life. None of you had the right to lock me out."

She glanced at the clipping still clutched in Ethan's grasp. A photo of a cryptic circle was half-visible beneath the headline. Her mind spun with possibilities. A wave of fury surged, tangling with sorrow.

Turning on her heel, she strode out of the sitting room. The hallway lights glimmered in her peripheral vision. She heard Ethan call her name again, his footsteps quick behind her. Her body shook as she rushed toward the door, tears threatening to spill.

CHAPTER
TWENTY

THE BRIDGE

Ivy sat alone on the highest ledge of the old observatory, where the broken dome once sheltered an ancient telescope. Moisture clung to the stone walls, and the Pacific's wind ruffled her hair, turning it into a restless curtain around her face. She drew her knees up and wrapped her arms around them, letting a chill seep into her bones. Out here, she felt the fullness of her anger and sorrow. It was nearly dusk, though the sun remained hidden behind a swath of ash-gray clouds. The fog hovered at the cliffs below, churning in slow circles that reminded her of her own spiraling thoughts.

She had fled from Cassandra's townhouse hours ago, footsteps echoing on slick pavement as she had practically run to the bus stop. Soon after, she had ended up at this remote vantage point north of the city, stepping wordlessly along the crumbled trail until she reached this place. The decommissioned observatory was a childhood haunt, a site where the old wooden beams and chipped stone seemed to watch over the restless ocean. In her youth, she and Robin would sneak up here to share secrets. The thick walls and high windows had once felt like a shield.

Now, as the evening light faded, she gazed into the mist below. A solemn feeling clung to the air, and for a brief moment, she almost convinced herself that she was the only person in existence. She closed her eyes, hoping the quiet would cradle her like it used to when she was younger. Her heart still throbbed from the argument. She felt betrayed by Ethan for digging up secrets without telling her, and by Cassandra for withholding so many crucial truths. The mention of a mysterious death in the past, an event Cassandra had witnessed, had torn open a wound Ivy did not realize she had. She pressed a palm to her chest, trying to slow her breathing.

She could not deny that she still cared deeply for Ethan. A large part of her missed him, but the trust they had tried to build now felt frayed at the edges. She shivered. The image of his eyes, sharp with both regret and resolve, lingered beneath her closed lids. That guilt deepened when she thought about Cassandra. Her aunt's reticence was maddening, as if she believed knowledge itself was a poison. Perhaps Cassandra's choices had been shaped by old horrors, but from Ivy's perspective, secrets only caused everything to rot from within. She rubbed the heel of her palm across her eyes, uncertain whether she was staving off tears or simply trying to push back the wave of exhaustion. The power that sometimes pricked beneath her skin felt distant here, as though the aged stone and drifting fog formed an impenetrable cocoon.

She drew a shaky breath, listening to the ocean hiss far below. It was at this very observatory that she realized her visions were not constant. Sometimes she would close her eyes here and sense only a soft, welcoming darkness. This was a place still mapped in her memory as safe. The sound of cautious footsteps across gravel pulled her from her thoughts. She lifted her chin, though she did not straighten her posture. She already knew who it would be. There was only one person who would guess where she had run.

Robin came through the gaping hole where a door used to be. They paused inside, slender shoulders outlined by the filtering twilight. Their cheeks looked slightly flushed from the trek along the cliffside path. Concern, tinted with relief, softened their gaze. They brushed a bit of dust off their leggings and cautiously picked their way across the debris-strewn floor.

"You're lucky I still remember how to get here," Robin said, voice pitched low. "It's darker than I remember. The path nearly ate my ankle."

Ivy managed a lopsided smile that did not reach her eyes. "It's rotten, no question," she murmured.

Robin nodded, eyes shifting around the hollowed structure, the crumbling scaffolding that ran around the dome's edges. The rotting wood smelled of salt, mildew, and the faintest trace of stale memories. Ivy recalled that when they were younger, the two of them would climb to the second story and sprawl out in sleeping bags to watch the stars through a broken half of the roof. They had believed those nights contained infinite potential.

"Seriously though, Ivy." Robin's voice cut through her recollection. "You never answered my texts. I got worried."

Ivy exhaled, shifting her gaze back to the ocean fog. "I'm sorry," she said softly. "I just..."

Her words trailed off.

Robin crouched near her, then eased onto a dusty stone ledge. For a moment, neither spoke. The hiss of the wind through broken windows served as the only backdrop. Ivy noticed how Robin's expression dipped between worry and quiet understanding. They were good at reading her, better than most. She forced a wry smile. "Remember back when we were fifteen? We'd sneak out, lugging flashlights and cheap snacks, swearing we'd see a ghost or a shooting star. Most nights, we found neither."

Robin's mouth curved in a gentle grin. "Yeah. But we listened to each other's weird dreams, borderline insane crushes, and everything else that felt overwhelming. Like now, except we're older and the stakes are a thousand times heavier."

Ivy's laugh came out small but real. "Yes. Now the weird dreams are psychic visions, and the borderline insane crush... well..." She paused, swallowing the sudden ache that rose in her chest at the thought of Ethan. "Maybe everything is complicated in ways I never expected."

Robin pressed a warm hand against Ivy's shoulder. "You're allowed to feel spilled-open and raw. It's been a wild ride." Robin's voice softened. "Tell me how you really feel, though. Let me help carry it."

She closed her eyes, letting the next breath linger in

her lungs like a raft on stormy seas. Cold wind grazed her cheeks. "I feel like I can't trust anyone," she admitted. "And I hate that. I've always wanted to see the best in people. But now I can't tell if I'm being naive. Ethan." Her breath caught. "I understood him better when he was merely a cynical reporter, but now I have all these... hopes for us. And Cassandra, she's my aunt, but I still can't untangle what she's hiding."

Robin nodded, letting Ivy's words sink in before responding. "I think Cassandra's secrecy is more about her own fears than a reflection of how she feels about you. She believes she's protecting you. She might be wrong, but she's not malicious. As for Ethan..." They sighed quietly, tapping a marble chunk sticking out from under the dusty floor. "I don't doubt he regrets how he handled that article. He's always been more comfortable with facts and evidence, even if that means bulldozing delicate territory."

Ivy's throat tightened. She had told herself she was furious with Ethan, yet when Robin put it plainly, she realized anger was only part of it. The deeper part was heartbreak, the instinctual fear that Ethan's thirst for a story would always eclipse her need for honesty and partnership. She turned her face away, letting the wind sting her eyes.

They sat in silence for another moment, warmed by the memory of better days and each other's presence. Slowly, Robin inched closer until they were side by side. Their shoulders nearly touched, two shapes huddled in the gloom of the old observatory. At last, Robin said, "I know I can't fix what happened. But I can remind you who you are, and that you're not alone. Sometimes in chaos, we forget."

Ivy's lips twitched. "Trust me, I'd love a reminder."

Robin reached over, taking Ivy's hand gently. "You are fierce," Robin said, voice low but strong. "You have a gift that can terrify, yes, but it can also protect and heal if you let it. You love deeply, even when it scares you. And you are never, ever undeserving of love."

An unsteady warmth spread through Ivy's chest. She did not respond at first, simply letting the realization settle.

She cleared her throat, hoping her voice would not break. "Thank you. It's hard... not to see myself as a harbinger of trouble. This gift, or curse, whichever it is, there's so much I don't understand."

"That doesn't disqualify you from love," Robin said firmly.

A seagull cried somewhere in the fog, and Ivy listened to the mournful echo drift along the wind. She wondered if she could ever harness her power in a way that felt safe. For that matter, she wondered if Ethan might still stand by her side when the dust cleared. She was furious with him, but she also missed him.

The distant glimmer of headlights shone along the coastal highway behind them, visible through cracks in the disintegrating wall. It reminded her that the world was still turning, the traffic humming through the city even as she stewed in her heartbreak.

Robin shifted, brushing some grit off the ledge. Their presence exuded. The decrepit wooden support beams overhead creaked a little, resonating through the structure. What followed was not quite comfortable, not quite tense. Ivy's mind wandered to the nights she had spent here in the past, desperate for silence from her visions. Back then, she had believed if she stayed in that silence, maybe the visions would vanish permanently. Now, ironically, she longed for clarity.

Robin slowly stood, walked a couple of paces around the ledge before returning, arms crossed for warmth. "Well," they said lightly, "if we stay much longer, we'll probably freeze. I guess that would solve some problems, if we turned into statue-people. But it might be inconvenient in the long run."

Ivy smirked softly. A wisp of humor cut through the gloom in her chest. "Statues wouldn't have to worry about heartbreak or betrayals."

"True. We also wouldn't get to experience coffee, or hugging our friends, or feeling the sun on our face." Robin's voice warmed. "No thanks."

A faint chuckle escaped Ivy as she carefully rose, mindful of the dust and broken planks. She glanced down at the ocean once more, noticing how the fog swelled like living breath. Soon, the darkness would deepen, and she did not relish the thought of stumbling back down the winding path with no flashlight. She brushed her palms against her jeans, letting out a slow exhale. Robin shifted closer. In the lingering quiet, their eyes met, and Ivy felt a small surge of gratitude that she did not need to be wholly alone. No matter how complicated life grew, Robin's steadfast loyalty remained a constant.

She let her gaze wander to the broken-down doorway ahead, the same threshold they had crossed many times in their youth. It beckoned now, signaling a path back to the city, back to a conversation that eventually needed to happen, back to truths that still needed facing. She was not ready tonight, but the knowledge weighed less heavily with Robin nearby. Finally, she turned to walk with Robin toward the old steps. There was a sense of unspoken agreement to linger only a moment longer, hearts beating in sync with the ocean. The air tasted of brine, and the rhythmic crash of distant waves provided an odd comfort.

Robin slowed, then settled onto the broken stone foundation once more, motioning for Ivy to do the same. Their expression was pensive. Ivy sank down onto a patch of stone next to them, feeling the weight of fatigue drape across her shoulders. She heard Robin swallow softly. "You came here a lot," they said, sitting beside her.

Ivy stared out. "It was the only place my visions stopped." Robin gently placed a hand over hers.

"You don't have to choose between being powerful and being loved."

Ivy finally looked at them. "But what if I'm not meant to be loved?"

"Tough luck. You already are." Robin smirked, their expression soft and sure.

TWENTY-ONE

THE RETURN

Ivy stood in the narrow alleyway behind her shop, breathing in the crisp air of early evening. A few hours had passed since she had last spoken to anyone. She felt more at peace out here. That was when her phone rang. She pulled it from her jacket and glanced at the screen, heart flipping when she recognized Cassandra's number. It had been so long since they last parted with anger and hurt roiling between them. She pressed Accept.

"Ivy," Cassandra said. The single word was gentle, almost hesitant.

Ivy leaned back against the old brick wall. "I'm here," she answered in a tight voice.

"Come to my house tonight," Cassandra said at last. "I would like to see you. We have... unfinished matters to discuss."

Ivy's pulse fluttered. She was caught between wariness and the love she still felt for her aunt, a love that had been tested lately. "Are you sure?"

"I am," Cassandra replied. "No questions asked... but I hope you'll come."

The line went silent. Ivy stared at her phone, mind racing. She slipped the device back into her pocket. Perhaps, she thought, it was finally time to have the conversation she had both dreaded and craved.

Later that evening, she hailed a rideshare and watched the city lights blur past. San Francisco's fog pressed against the windows as the car wove between glowing intersections. Each time the driver slowed, Ivy wondered if she should simply ask him to take her back to her apartment instead. Fear whispered that she was not ready to face Cassandra's confession, while another part of her insisted that she needed closure. When the driver pulled up at Cassandra's ivy-covered townhouse, Ivy climbed out and gazed upward at the tall windows, nearly all of them dim. Only a faint gleam of orange glowed behind heavy curtains on the second floor. She felt as though she were walking into a realm removed from time, where leftover echoes of secrets waited.

She climbed the front steps, noticing the old wooden door was slightly ajar. The evening fog slipped in around her ankles as she stepped inside. The entry hallway smelled of incense, like jasmine laced with something heavier, something that spoke of old magic. She remembered the many times she had visited this place in search of answers, only to walk away with more questions. *How different would tonight be?* Cassandra appeared at the end of the hallway, wearing a flowing wrap the color of midnight. Her thin braids were coiled into a low knot at the nape of her neck. Shadows danced across her face, cast by a single lantern in her hand. For a moment, neither of them spoke.

"Thank you for coming," Cassandra said. Her voice held a softness Ivy was not used to hearing.

Ivy managed a nod. "You asked, so I came."

They looked at each other. Cassandra turned and gestured for Ivy to follow. She led her through a short hallway into a sitting room lit only by the warm glow of a fire in the old hearth. The layered carpets muffled the sound of Ivy's boots as she made her way inside. Soft golden light rested over shelves of books half-obscured by drifting smoke from an incense stick.

A pair of worn armchairs waited by the fire. Cassandra lowered herself into one, placing the lantern on a side table. She patted the other chair in invitation. Ivy sank down carefully, bracing for whatever Cassandra had to say. She tucked her hands into her lap and let the heat of the fire warm her cheeks.

They stared at the dancing flames for a few moments before Cassandra broke the stillness. "I have not done enough," she said. "I know that. I should have been honest with you from the start. I should have protected you better, yet I ran. I ran because I feared what I saw in you."

Ivy frowned. She folded her arms, pressing them against the subtle ache that rose in her chest. "Feared what exactly?"

Cassandra exhaled, shoulders drooping. "When you were born, I felt a strange shift in the currents of power that reach through our bloodline. I had visions, glimpses of two very different futures for you. In one, you died far too young. In the other... you became something beyond what I could comprehend, someone with staggering power. And sometimes, when I glimpsed that version of you, I wasn't certain it was you at all. It scared me. I did not know which path would unfold, or if my involvement would tip the scales."

Ivy recalled how Cassandra had vanished from her life when she was still small, visiting only sporadically. Growing up, she believed her aunt was too busy or simply uninterested in a normal family dynamic. Ivy swallowed. "You left because you were afraid you would cause one of those futures to happen?"

Cassandra nodded, pressing her palms together over her lap. Her eyes reflected the fireplace. "Seeing those outcomes shook me, child. I felt trapped, as if by guiding you, I might accidentally seal your doom. And by ignoring your potential, I might allow you to bloom into something unstoppable. I couldn't bear that choice."

Ivy sat speechless. Outside, the wind pressed gently against the old house.

"So, you chose not to be there for me at all," Ivy said quietly.

Cassandra lowered her gaze. "I told myself it was mercy. I told myself that if I stayed away, you would find your own path, free of my influence. I justified my absence by thinking that if fate wanted you to awaken, you would do so on your own. I thought it wasn't my place to interfere."

The fire crackled, and a log collapsed into embers,

sending sparks into the air. Ivy realized she was trembling slightly. She thought of the lonely nights she had spent, confused by the strange images in her mind. If Cassandra had been honest, would Ivy's journey have been less harrowing? "You were supposed to be the one person who understood," she murmured. "Instead, you left me to figure it out alone."

Cassandra's glance shot upward. Lines of sorrow threaded her features. "And I have regretted that ever since."

They lapsed into silence. Ivy rubbed the pad of her thumb over the edge of the chair's armrest. She considered the disappointments, vexations, and heartbreak that had piled on ever since she had begun accepting her gift. Yet a faint sense of relief rolled over her at hearing Cassandra's truths. It helped to know Cassandra's aloofness had come from fear, not apathy.

Cassandra shifted, leaning forward. "Ivy," she said gently, "I know my apology can't erase the harm. But you need to understand, power is not a simple birthright. It shapes everyone around it. I was terrified that pushing you toward it would devour you. Or that letting you stumble aimlessly would destroy you. The burden I carried was the knowledge that I might influence your entire fate."

Ivy stared at the flames. She recalled how she had once longed for a mentor. Now that mentor sat across from her, gazing with regret. She exhaled and asked the question circling her thoughts.

"Are you still afraid I'll become something dreadful?" Her voice was small, betraying her anxiety.

Cassandra sighed. "I am not convinced that your power is malevolent, nor that it will destroy you. You are neither wholly light nor wholly darkness, child. And your gifts are not anchored in a single path if you choose to shape them. But the risk remains that if you are pushed too far, or if you choose the wrong alliances, your abilities could become more than you or I can contain."

Ivy's jaw tightened. "You've warned me many times," she said, "but too often, your warnings were riddles. I can't live my life obeying fears you once glimpsed. I need to decide my own course."

Cassandra allowed a small, weary smile. "I suppose I deserve that."

Silence fell again, broken only by the crackle of burning wood. Ivy closed her eyes for a moment, letting the warmth of the fire seep into her. She recalled the illusions, the arguments, and the fierce sense of betrayal. All that might remain, but at least tonight had delivered clarity.

Ivy spoke, her voice gentle but resolute. "I'm done running from what I am. I'm not here to be anyone's prophecy, and I refuse to live in fear of a future that may or may not happen. I'm here to choose my own path."

She lifted her gaze to meet Cassandra's eyes. She expected more warnings. Instead, Cassandra nodded, her expression thoughtful. "You speak like you truly mean it," she said. "That conviction is part of your strength, Ivy. Use it well."

Ivy swallowed, unsure why tears threatened to fall. The relief of hearing genuine acceptance from Cassandra left her feeling both light and bruised. Despite the tension between them, she did not sense further resentment, only a mutual longing to bridge the gap that haunted them. She shifted her weight, inhaling the comforting scent of jasmine incense as it mingled with the smoky undertone of the fire.

"Where... where have you been all this time?" Ivy asked softly. "I know you didn't disappear entirely, but you never stayed."

Cassandra's features tightened. She glanced into the fire. "I tried to distract myself with traveling, to New Orleans, to small gatherings of other seers, pretending I could outrun the knowledge of what you may become. In truth, none of it made me feel better. The more distance I put between us, the heavier my guilt grew. I always kept an eye on you anyway, through people I trusted or through my old connections in this city. I never stopped watching." Her voice trembled.

Ivy remembered how she had spotted Cassandra in fleeting glimpses at some of the city's esoteric fairs, though always at a distance.

"I won't say it was the right choice," Cassandra added. "It was simply the one I made out of fear. I cannot change that, but I can promise to do differently now. If you'll allow it."

Ivy pressed her lips together. The old hurt still ached, but an ember of understanding began to glow inside her. She recognized a bit of herself in Cassandra's decisions, that urge to shut everyone out. Perhaps they were more alike than she cared to admit.

Finally, she nodded, the movement tentative but genuine. "If you want to be here," she said, "I won't turn you away."

A faint breath of relief passed through Cassandra's lips. She rose from her chair and opened a narrow cabinet in the corner of the room. She slipped out a thin, leather-bound journal, worn at the edges. The cover was a deep shade of burgundy.

Turning, Cassandra handed the journal to Ivy. Her gaze lingered on the old book before she spoke. "I started writing in this shortly after you were born," she said. "I documented every time I felt a surge of power around you, every unusual moment. When I left, I took it with me, thinking maybe I would find answers in the patterns. I never did. But I think it's time you read it yourself. There may be parts that help you understand not only me, but how far back your gifts go."

TWENTY-TWO

THE KISS

I vy exhaled a sigh of relief as the bell above the shop door chimed, signaling the departure of her last customer. She offered a parting smile from behind the small wooden counter. The two candles burning on the front table sent wavering shadows across the floor, and the overlapping scents of lavender and sandalwood hung in the air. She thought about snuffing them out but decided to wait. The shop felt peaceful in that dusky glow.

She turned to her tarot table, where a few cards lay scattered. The Fool and the Lovers. The customer had requested guidance on a relationship. Now that the session was over, she carefully gathered the cards and straightened them. Though she tried to keep her mind on the routine, she could not shake her own turmoil. She felt as if she carried a splinter in her chest, lodged deep enough that simple logic would not remove it.

A knock broke the stillness. She stilled, listening as it

sounded again, a dull rap on the door's stained glass panel. It was after closing, and she normally would not answer, but her curiosity stirred. She moved to the front and peered through the glass. She saw a man's silhouette, broad shoulders and a familiar tilt of the head. Her heart jolted. Ethan stood in the doorway, wearing a fatigue on his expression that nearly broke her heart. She drew a breath, bracing herself. Her hand settled on the lock, and for an instant she debated leaving him outside. The memory of their recent arguments flooded her mind. Gently, she turned the key and opened the door.

He gazed at her with remorse in his eyes. "Ivy," he said, stepping over the threshold. "I know it's late. I messed up, but I needed to see you." His voice was raw, as though he had already rehearsed a dozen apologies on his way here.

She clenched her jaw, wrangling the emotion inside her. "You messed up," she repeated in a calm tone, "because you were so fixated on secrets that you forgot there was a person behind them." Her chest felt tight, but she refused to look down. She crossed her arms, a small shield against the warmth of him standing so close.

He nodded, eyes moving to the floor before meeting her gaze again. "You have every right to be angry. I never lied about wanting to understand you, though." His voice shook. "I only... I went about it the wrong way."

Ivy's throat constricted. She found herself teetering on the razor's edge between vulnerability and anger. "You do not get to declare that you want to understand me," she said, her words precise, "as though I'm some myth you can unravel."

His shoulders tensed. "That's not what I meant," he murmured, sliding his hands into his jacket pockets. Even that gesture seemed laced with caution. "I want you, not your story." He stopped, searching her face.

She felt the weight of his confession. He had once promised to be an ally, but his methods had cut deep. She was unsure if she could believe him. Yet she wanted to.

Without warning, she turned and moved behind the counter, pretending to gather scattered items. She heard his footstep on the creaking floorboard near the threshold, but he did not follow. The distance between them felt both too wide and too narrow.

She set the tarot deck on a faded velvet cloth, then faced him. "Let's lay it out," she said, quiet anger in her tone. "You already doubt me sometimes. I doubt you too. Is there a point to this conversation?"

Ethan raked a hand through his hair. She caught the movement of his throat as he swallowed. "There is a point," he said, voice low. "Because neither of us seems able to walk away. Or am I wrong?"

She had no easy answer, so she glared at him instead. "I can't shrug off what happened. I felt used, Ethan." Her stomach twisted. "And maybe I'm being foolish for letting you in at all."

His expression darkened with regret. "I never wanted you to feel used," he voiced. "I chased answers because I was afraid you'd get hurt. There were things about your family, your aunt... you were in danger." He paused. "Until recently, I only knew how to handle danger by investigating it. I never meant to push you away."

For a moment, the only sound was the faint crackle of the candles on the counter. Ivy's entire body felt rigid.

At last, she forced out a breath. "Tell me why you are here tonight."

He took a careful step closer. She observed the tired lines etched around his eyes. "Because I miss you," he said. "And because I don't want us to end like this. I made mistakes, but they were never about lying to you. I just... I needed to make sense of everything without scaring you."

"Scaring me?" she echoed, bristling. "I can handle quite a bit, in case you have not noticed."

He nodded slowly. "You absolutely can. Sometimes I forget you are stronger than you look."

Her anger flared hotter. She put both hands on the countertop. "Don't patronize me."

Ethan's breath caught. He moved around the counter, and Ivy stiffened. She did not back away, though she felt the tension between them spark like electricity. "I'm not patronizing you," he said softly. "I've seen you stand your ground when anyone else would have run."

She sensed him pausing, as though asking for permission to get nearer. Her arms relaxed at her sides. He took one more step, until only a sliver of air stood between them. In that moment, the incense, melting candle wax, and his subtle cologne seemed to merge all at once.

His voice turned quiet. "Ivy... if you want me to leave, say the word."

She swallowed. The memory of their last argument stung. Now his nearness made her pulse race. She was furious at him. She was drawn to him. She hated that she could not decide. Then came the silence. He lifted a hand as if to touch her cheek, but he did not make contact. He waited, searching her expression for some sign of acceptance or rejection. Ivy's anger raged, but behind it pooled a longing she could not deny.

She released a spiraling breath. "If I tell you to leave," she whispered, "will you?"

"Yes," he replied, voice hoarse.

She closed her eyes, letting a wave of conflicting emotions wash over her. Her fingertips twitched with the urge to grab his collar and pull him closer, to forget her hurt in the warmth of his arms. She could not cast him out. Not tonight. When she remained silent, he stepped in, angling himself until their chests nearly touched. Gently, he pressed his forehead against hers. His breath came shallow.

"Then tell me to leave," he repeated, a near-whisper.

Ivy opened her eyes, meeting his. She saw the vestiges of heartbreak there, the quiet desperation that echoed her own. Before her voice could betray her, she closed the distance with a hesitant kiss. The contact was so soft that at first it felt like testing a bruise, seeing if the pain was still there. It was. A pang of memory, of doubt, of missed chances. Yet beneath it all was a tenderness that had never disappeared.

She could taste the salt of her own unshed tears. His lips lingered for a heartbeat longer before they both pulled back an inch, breath mingling. She saw him exhale shakily, and her heart clenched. He kissed her again, slow and deliberate, as if he feared one wrong move might shatter everything. Ivy felt her pulse thrum wildly in her ears. The outside world fell away, replaced by the warmth of his body and the soft glow of the shop's candlelit air. Eventually, she shifted back and touched the side of her mouth, startled by how her lips still tingled. She looked at him, arms unfolding. They both seemed winded, vulnerable. "I do not know how to forgive you," she admitted. "Or if I can yet."

He nodded. "I'm not asking for immediate forgiveness," he said gently. "Just a chance to show you why I care."

They stood in fragile agreement for a moment, neither sure of the next step. Finally, she inhaled. "I was about to close up," she said.

Ethan glanced at the burning candles that created dancing shadows on the walls. "I could help you lock up, if that's all right," he offered.

She felt a mix of relief and anxiety. Still, she nodded. "Okay," she said softly, turning away to snuff out one of the candles. Once the flame vanished, the space felt darker, but somehow more comforting. She lifted the second candle, intending to carry it into the back room.

Ethan's hand trailed lightly along her elbow, a tentative gesture that asked permission to stay close. She led him toward the shelves behind the curtain that separated the shop's main area from the cramped storage. The small room glowed in the single candle's light. She set the candle on a stack of empty boxes, then met his gaze again.

They had always been opposites. Her quiet caution alongside his driven pursuit of truth. Yet in certain moments, she had felt they fit perfectly, like pieces of cloth cut from the same pattern of longing. Tonight, the edges were still jagged, but there was an undeniable pull.

She spoke quietly. "Would you like some wine? I have a bottle I keep here for... when the day is rougher than usual."

Ethan's shoulders loosened. "Yes," he said. "That would be nice."

She retrieved the bottle and found two mismatched mugs. Pouring the deep crimson liquid, she passed him one. They leaned against a dusty bookshelf in silence. The tension eased a fraction with each sip. Ivy let the wine's warmth coat her tongue, calming the frayed edges of her nerves.

He studied her face. At last, he ventured softly, "What are you thinking?"

She swirled the wine. "How I'm not sure when trust became so fragile. I hate feeling guarded around you."

He nodded, taking a measured sip. "I do too," he admitted. "But maybe it's better to feel guarded than to stop caring."

Ivy exhaled a shaky breath, conceding the point with a small incline of her head. They settled into an uneven calm, punctuated by occasional gulps of wine and hesitant exchange of glances. The candle in the back room had burned low, sending a faint trail of smoke skyward. Time felt suspended. Eventually, she put her mug aside and set a hand on his shoulder. A longing and caution tugged at her. She leaned in, capturing his mouth in another slow kiss. This time, it was heavier with regret, yet grounded in the spark that had always flared between them. He made a quiet sound in his throat, drawing her closer.

When they broke apart, they each stood breathing hard. Ivy pressed her forehead to his collarbone and let herself remain there, letting the rise and fall of his breathing ground her. Even if her heart felt bruised, the warmth of his arms was an undeniable comfort. Minutes blurred. Soon, they were back in the main area, snuffing another candle and exchanging a murmured laugh when Ivy nearly burned her fingertip on the hot wick. He caught her hand and kissed the spot gently. He checked his watch and frowned. "It's late," he said reluctantly.

She inhaled. She had never resolved to let him remain here, but there was a small ache at the thought of him leaving. "Maybe that's enough for one night," she said, voice soft.

He brushed a thumb over her cheek. "I'll go if that is what you want."

She nodded, not quite able to speak the heartbreak that still lingered. "We both need some rest," she managed.

He lowered his hand. They walked to the door, and she unlocked it. On the threshold, he paused, turning to cup her jaw one last time.

She kissed him again, a final, lingering press of lips that made her stomach flutter. "Good night," she whispered.

His eyes held a promise. "Good night, Ivy."

He walked out into the cool darkness, and she quietly locked the door behind him. Leaning her forehead against the worn wood, she heard his footsteps fade. The candles still carried a faint glow. With the taste of wine and uncertainty on her tongue, she flipped the sign to Closed and walked slowly back inside, ready to extinguish the last flame before going home.

TWENTY-THREE

THE ECHO II

Ivy woke to darkness so complete it felt like velvet pressed against her eyes. Her breathing came in shallow, panicked waves, and she clutched at the sheets as she forced herself to remember where she was. Slowly, she recognized the familiar shadows of her bedroom. She searched over the dim outline of the windows and the faint glow of the streetlamp filtering through the curtains. This was her apartment, and she was safe, or at least safer than she felt in the vision.

Her heart still pounded. She had seen herself at five years old, crouched on creaking floorboards. Light and dust brushed her cheeks as she rummaged in a small dark space beneath those boards. She sensed a child's excitement at having a private secret. The memory carried a warmth she rarely found in her visions. But something changed in the last moment, when the vision twisted from simple nostalgia to an ominous flare of fear. She could almost hear voices approaching from somewhere above her. Then it had all vanished.

She sat there, her back digging into the headboard, a damp sheen across her forehead. Her throat felt dry. Finally, she whispered the words that had burst from her lips upon waking.

"It is still there."

She did not understand how she felt so certain. But the memory of tiny fingers lifting a board and stashing something inside burned bright in her mind. If she reached out, it was as almost as though she could touch it. She exhaled, pushing the wild tangle of hair from her face. This was not a prophecy of doom. It was something quietly personal and oddly urgent.

For several minutes, she stared at the ceiling, too restless to lie back down. Echoes of the dream gnawed at her. Could childhood illusions truly remain hidden for this long? She thought about the uneasy dinners at her parent's house. She recalled how her mother would freeze if Ivy mentioned seeing things that did not align with the rational world Anna Lewis demanded. Could it be that her younger self had tried to conceal evidence of her budding gift? She wanted answers, but the mere idea of delving into that old house while her parents were there made her stomach clench.

As the night wore on, she gave up on sleep. She padded to the kitchen and made tea. The whir of the electric kettle set a soft, grounding undertone to her thoughts. She cradled the warm mug in her palms and allowed the light scent of chamomile to soothe her sporadic shivers. Her aunt Cassandra had once said that every vision, even a gentle one, arrived for a reason.

Ivy did not want to interpret it alone. By habit, she glanced at her phone on the counter, the screen dark. Calling Ethan at this hour would be selfish. He had left her shop only recently, and the simmering tension between them still tingled. Yet she longed to hear his voice. She ran her thumb over her phone's screen, hesitating. Finally, she placed it face down on the counter. She could wait until morning.

When dawn broke, Ivy was sitting at her small table by the window, half-drowsy and wrapped in one of her thick sweaters. She jumped a little when her phone buzzed. Glancing at it, she saw a short message from Ethan.

"Morning. Are you all right?"

She released an unsteady breath. Somehow, he always seemed to sense her moods. After last night's dream, it felt good to see him checking in. She texted back in a more casual tone than she felt. "Barely slept. Can we meet? I have to tell you something."

He replied quickly, suggesting a café near The Oracle. Ivy's stomach fluttered in anticipation, and the worry that had coiled in her muscles all night shifted into relief. Maybe talking about the dream with someone who believed her would help her unravel its meaning.

She arrived at the café to find Ethan already seated by the window, long fingers curled around a mug of black coffee. His hair was a bit tousled, as though it was hastily combed with the edge of his hand. The space thrummed with the low hum of conversation and the scent of hot espresso.

"Hey," he said softly, standing halfway as if to greet her, then remembering the other patrons. He settled back down and gestured for her to sit. She sighed, realizing how exhausted she must appear. Sliding onto the chair opposite him, she took in his practiced calm.

"Did you get any sleep?" he asked, giving her a narrowed look.

"Not really," she said. "I had another vision, but it was... different. Not some tragedy or terrifying sign." She paused to let the words gather shape on her tongue. "It was me as a child, in my old bedroom at my parents' place."

He adjusted his posture, leaning closer. "Your bedroom? And it felt real, like a memory, not a nightmare?"

She nodded. "I was around five years old. I was crawling under loose floorboards. It seemed like I was hiding something there, something I didn't want my parents to see. At first, I felt happy, like I was guarding a treasure. Then everything shifted, and there was fear. I heard footsteps above me, but the dream ended before I saw whose they were."

He watched her with that intense gaze that had once unsettled her. Today, it encouraged her to keep going. "Do you have any idea what you were hiding?"

Her throat tightened. "No. It was a feeling more than an item. The sense that I was protecting something important. Maybe something that proved my visions weren't daydreams, even back then. I can't explain why, but I woke up certain it is still there, under those same floorboards."

He rapped his knuckles softly against the table, lost in thought. "Have you mentioned anything like this to your parents? Or your aunt?"

Ivy swallowed. "No. I'm not sure my aunt would know. But my mother..." Her lips curved in a humorless smile. "She would probably dismiss it. She always believed I needed therapy whenever I said I saw something strange. She would never have wanted me stashing anything that reaffirmed my gift."

Ethan set a hand on the table, palm up in invitation. "We should look for it ourselves. You said your parents are out of town soon?"

Her breath hitched. "They are leaving for a conference this weekend. My mother asked me to water the plants. I was going to ignore that request." She gave a weak laugh. "But maybe this is the perfect time."

He nodded, expression resolute. "I'll go with you. We can check under those boards and see if you did leave something behind. If it's nothing, at least we can say we tried."

His calm certainty made her chest tighten with gratitude. She had expected him to question her. Instead, he had accepted her dream with an unwavering willingness to help. This was what trust felt like.

"Thank you," she murmured, letting her own hand inch across the table until her fingertips brushed his. The contact sent a sliver of warmth through her arm, almost balancing the chill that had haunted her since she woke up.

They both grew silent while the café bustled around them. A server passed by to refill Ethan's coffee. The clink of cups and low chatter formed a comforting background hum. Outside, the sun peeked through a layer of morning fog, making the windows glow faintly.

"How are you feeling?" he asked, once the server left.

Her gaze shifted to the steam rising from his coffee. "I'm uneasy," she admitted. "I've been preparing myself for big visions, warnings of danger. But this... it felt so personal. It was like unearthing a lost part of myself. I'm worried about what it means."

He studied her for a long moment. "Sometimes the things that matter most are the hidden threads in our own past," he said. "Maybe you need closure there too." Then he offered a small, hesitant smile. "And we can water your parents' plants, so at least you're fulfilling the request."

Her lips curved weakly. "Right. Priorities." She rubbed the heel of her hand over one eye, exhaustion still tugging at her. "I have a bad feeling that if we do find something, it might open questions I'm not ready to face."

"We'll face them together," Ethan said softly.

She nodded, not quite trusting herself to speak. Emotions lodged in her throat, equal parts anticipation and dread. She had shut off so many memories from childhood. Maybe uncovering them would help piece together her fractured sense of identity. Or maybe it would confirm her mother's worst fear, that Ivy's gift had been blossoming long before she had the language to describe it.

Their plan took shape quickly. They agreed to meet two days from now, a Saturday, and head to her parents' house after midday. Her parents' flight would depart early, which gave them a window of time to investigate without risking an unexpected confrontation.

She hesitated, pen still poised. "I'm going to pack a flashlight," she said suddenly. "That crawl space is probably dusty and dark."

Ethan nodded. "Good thinking. I'll bring a couple of items from my recording gear, in case we need extra light."

Ivy arched an eyebrow, a small hint of amusement in her eyes. "You intend to record me rummaging around under my old bedroom floor?"

"I like to be prepared," he said, and the corners of his mouth lifted. "Old habits. You never know what we might find."

She could not argue. Despite the tangle of her feelings, she found a glimmer of relief knowing he stood ready to help.

They finished their coffees, talking over mundane details. The conversation carried an undercurrent of unspoken tension, as if they were both aware that rummaging through her childhood could tear open more than old floorboards. Ivy kept noticing the subtle lines of concern crossing Ethan's face every time their gazes locked, as though he wanted to ask if she truly felt strong enough to do this. She did not know what answer she would give, except that she could not ignore the vision any longer.

When they stood to leave, he placed a hand gently on

her shoulder. "You can text me if you have more dreams, or if you can't sleep," he said.

She managed a small nod, her pulse fluttering in her throat. "I will," she promised. She thanked him softly. He gave her one more searching glance, then followed her out to the sidewalk. Morning sunlight had burned away much of the fog. People bustled past, some with cups of coffee clenched in their hands, others with briefcases or strolling dogs. The city moved on as though it had no inkling of the quiet puzzle stirring inside Ivy's mind.

As they made their goodbyes, Ethan lingered. "I'll see you soon," he said. It sounded less like a farewell and more like an affirmation of solidarity.

She nodded. "Yes. Soon."

He departed, leaving Ivy on the sidewalk, the day stretching before her in uncertain shades of possibility. She watched his figure disappear around a corner before finally letting out a long exhale. There was no immediate sense of danger. More like a faint humming, the call of memory.

She adjusted the strap of her purse and started walking back toward The Oracle. If her parents truly had no idea what lay beneath the floor of her childhood bedroom, or if they did and tried to hide it, this weekend would surely force some corners of the past into the open. Ivy's hands trembled at the thought of creeping into that house, rummaging under old boards, and confronting whatever her younger self had once believed was worth protecting.

Two days. That was all the time she had to gather her

nerves. She reminded herself that no matter what, she would not face it alone. Ethan would be there. Perhaps that was enough.

Still, a whisper of dread brushed the back of her mind, and she recalled how the vision ended. Her five-year-old self looking upward, heart pounding at the hint of approaching footsteps. Ivy did not yet know whose presence had frightened her all those years ago, but she had a feeling she was about to find out. And once she did, there would be no burying that secret again.

TWENTY-FOUR

THE BOX

Ivy held her breath on the creaking porch steps outside her parents' house. The night sky glowed faintly with distant city lights, and a breeze carried the scent of eucalyptus from the neighboring yard. She gripped a small flashlight, conscious of how her knuckles had gone white. Ethan stood behind her, leaning close enough that she could feel the gentle warmth of his breath against her hair.

"This is it," she whispered. She tried the front door. Locked. She glanced sideways at Ethan. "I should still have my old key."

He nodded, his own flashlight tucked in his jacket. "Let's hope your parents haven't changed the locks."

She fumbled in her purse. Though she had walked through this doorway countless times, it felt strange to arrive with the plan of searching for something hidden. There was a low hum of tension between them, as if the house itself held its breath. She found the key at last, an old tarnished piece of metal. Slipping it into the lock, she gave a gentle turn. The doorknob clicked. Relief trickled through her.

They stepped inside. The hollow thud of the door shutting seemed louder than she remembered, and Ivy paused to let her eyes adjust to the darkness. A wave of childhood memories fluttered. That familiar living room lamp, the sofa where she once hid after a nightmare, the scratch in the hardwood where she had once dropped a heavy bowl.

Ethan caught her tentative movement and placed a cautious hand on her shoulder. "We'll be quick. Your parents don't come back until Sunday morning, right?"

"That's what my mother told me," Ivy said, forcing her shoulders to relax. "They wanted me to water the plants." A shaky laugh threatened to spill from her. She was not here to do chores. She nodded toward the hallway. "My bedroom's upstairs."

Moving carefully, they walked across the silent living room. Familiar furniture loomed like silhouettes. The heavy armchair her father favored, the glass coffee table her mother kept immaculate. Ivy caught her reflection in the glass coffee table, faint and ghostly, then tore her eyes away. They reached the staircase. A wave of musty air greeted them. Her parents seldom used the upper floor since she moved out, aside from storing leftover boxes in the guest room. Every floorboard squeak made Ivy's skin prickle. At the top of the stairs, she paused in front of a narrow doorway. It had once been plastered with stickers and a small nameplate that read *Ivy*. Now only faint outlines remained. She rested her palm against the door.

Ethan leaned in, voice warm. "Take as long as you need."

She nodded. The knob turned easily, and they slipped inside. Ivy switched on her flashlight around her old bedroom. Dust motes danced in the glow, rising like tiny ghosts. The walls had been repainted a neutral beige, and the bed was gone. A few random boxes lined one corner, labeled "Ivy's stuff" in her mother's brisk handwriting. The rest of the space was eerily empty.

"Nothing's left," Ivy murmured. "My mother cleared out everything."

Ethan followed her gaze, shining his light along the worn hardwood floor. "We'll figure it out. You said you saw yourself under the boards?"

"Yes," she whispered. "And it felt so real. I remember the rough wood, dust on my fingers. I was, hiding something."

She dropped to one knee, heart thudding. She skimmed the flashlight across the floorboards until she spotted one with a slight warp. Shuffling over, she glanced up at Ethan. He set his own flashlight on the floor so its beam spilled sideways.

She levered her fingertips under the corner. The wood refused to budge at first, squeaking under her pull. With another careful tug, it loosened. A small cavity yawned beneath, dark and cramped. Ivy shone the flashlight inside. Cold air brushed her cheek. Something was wrapped in cloth inside, an oblong shape, maybe the size of a hardcover book. Her pulse spiked. Memories flashed. A child's stillness, the thrill of burying a secret. She slid the bundle out carefully. Ethan crouched next to her, brow furrowed in concentration. Together, they peeled away the faded gray material to reveal a small wooden box secured with a tarnished clasp. The box had the same faint odor of dust and old paper.

Ethan brushed a hand against her arm. "You okay?"

Ivy forced a nod. "Yes. Just, nervous. I don't know what I'm going to find."

She unlatched the box and lifted its lid. Immediately, she saw a stack of folded papers, aged around the edges. Not merely paper, she realized, but drawings. Charcoal lines and colored pencil scrawls. She set the box down, then gently lifted the top few sheets. Anxiety slid through her veins. She could not recall ever drawing these images.

Her flashlight slid across the first one. Flames. A figure stood in front of a backdrop of roaring red and orange. The lines were messy, clearly from a small child's hand, but the intensity jolted her. She swallowed, flipping to the next page. This one showed a group of people, no faces drawn, only silhouettes in some swirling chaos. Another drawing showed a skeletal shape that might have been a boat on stormy water, or a building collapsing. The edges were smudged.

Ethan shifted closer. "These are older," he murmured.

Ivy barely heard him. She flipped another page and froze. It was a portrait of a man, rendered far more carefully than the rest, detailed enough that the shape of his jaw, the arch of his eyebrows, and the faint shimmer of hair was hauntingly familiar.

Lucien Grey. She recognized him with a jarring certainty, even though she had never met him as a child. It was impossible. Yet here, scrawled in a child's shaky lines, was the image of that sharp face, eyes half-lidded with an almost amused expression. At the bottom, a name was written in uneven handwriting.

LUCIEN GREY.

Her heart hammered in her throat. She felt Ethan's breath catch. He studied the childish scrawl, then her face. "This is him," he whispered. "The one from your dream. The man who..."

She nodded, mouth dry. "I never knew I drew him. I never, remember any of this."

Ethan turned a fraction toward her, reaching to brush a strand of hair from her cheek. "It means you've been seeing things for longer than you realized. Do you think your parents...?"

Before he finished, Ivy lifted another page. The scrawls beneath it were more frantic. Beneath that page was the final item. A folded sheet of stationery. She recognized her mother's neat, no-nonsense handwriting on the outside. Ivy's wrists trembled with a surge of emotion.

Ethan's eyes moved from the stationery to her face. She slipped her finger under the fold. Carefully, she opened it. The letter was short.

I did this to protect you. You were so young. I didn't know what else to do. I hope one day you understand that I only wanted you safe, wanted you free.

I will always love you, Ivy.

No signature or date. Just that small message. Ivy realized her throat was so tight, she could barely swallow. She felt the weight of conflicting emotions. Confusion, betrayal, a spark of relief that her mother cared enough to try something. The letter did not clarify what her mother had done or why, only that she knew. She had always known

Ivy inhaled a shaky breath, reading it aloud so Ethan could hear. "I did this to protect you. You were so young... I hope one day you understand that I only wanted you safe... I will always love you, Ivy."

Her voice cracked on the last few words, tears threatening. She remembered countless times as a child when she would mention a strange dream only to have her mother quiet her. She pressed her fingertips to her eyes, swallowing the urge to sob. The house was still, the air thick. It felt as if her mother's presence lingered in every corner, watching.

"She knew," Ivy whispered finally, lowering the letter. Her gaze darted to the drawings again, especially the portrait of Lucien Grey.

Ethan's arm came around her shoulders, steady and warm. She let him cradle her close, a slight trembling in her limbs. The sound of the empty house pressed against her ears. She could almost imagine the younger version of herself creeping into this bedroom, dropping to her knees, carefully tucking away secrets she did not understand.

Ivy squeezed her eyes shut, the letter's words echoing. *Protect you.* Had her mother truly done it out of love? The half-resentment, half-grief that twisted in Ivy's chest left her dizzy. She remembered how, in the years that followed, she had tried so hard to rationalize the fleeting glimpses, the sudden knowledge she would glean. Now, the evidence lay before her. A child's scribbles predicting a face she should never have known. A name she could not possibly have heard. All hidden beneath the floor so she would not see the proof of her abilities. She opened her eyes and looked at Ethan. He studied her quietly, his expression shadowed with concern. He moved his thumb against her shoulder in a gentle circle.

"We came here to find answers," he said, voice soft. "But maybe this raises more questions."

She nodded, not trusting herself to speak. Carefully, she reached for the child's drawing of Lucien. The charcoal lines were smudged, but the eyes were undeniably his. Beneath the name, small phrases were scratched out, letters that overlapped to the point of illegibility. Her mother must have seen them, recognized something, and decided to hide it all away.

She exhaled, trying to steady the tremor in her voice. "I can't believe how many pages there are." She flipped through a few more drawings, each one of shapes or scenes she could not decipher. Some were haunting, with shadowy figures and half-formed words. Others looked like she had tried to draw normal childhood pictures of trees and houses, only to have the lines warp into strange forms. "I have no memory of making them."

"That means your gift was there all along," Ethan murmured. "Even if you didn't understand it."

She swallowed hard. "My mother must have known I'd never stop trying to see. She thought burying these would spare me."

The letter in her hand trembled. Perhaps her mother genuinely believed it was best for Ivy's future. Perhaps she resented that their household would never be normal.

"We should..." Ethan began, but he swallowed the words. Instead, he laid a hand over the letter, a gentle gesture of solidarity.

Ivy felt her lips press together. She wanted to know how long her mother had wrestled with this decision. The letter gave no timeline, only regret and hope. A pinprick of grief found its way into her heart. She recognized that her mother's brand of love was complicated, shaped by denial and fear. And though it hurt, it also felt oddly comforting that Anna had cared enough to do something.

She set the drawings back in the box, her eyes lingering on Lucien's face. "I need to keep these," she whispered, pressing the cloth gently around them. "They're part of who I was."

Ethan nodded. "Of course."

With slow care, she closed the lid. The house deepened, its old walls seeming to carry the weight of unspoken secrets. She kneeled in the dust of her childhood room, the letter limp in her hand, Ethan's arm a steady comfort. Somewhere deep in her chest, a mixture of dread and certainty mingled. Dread for whatever these drawings portended, for the shadow of Lucien Grey that had taunted her from childhood. Certainty, because the truth was finally coming to the surface, no matter how much it stung.

She whispered again, softer this time, "She knew. She always knew."

Silence fell. The letter fluttered as she set it on top of the box, the words burning in her mind. She glanced at Ethan, and he nodded gently. There was nothing more to say. They had found what they came for. And there, in the dim of her old bedroom, Ivy felt her world tilt on its axis once again.

TWENTY-FIVE

THE CHOICE

Ivy felt a heaviness descend the moment her feet crossed the threshold into her parents' home. The morning light slanted through the tall windows, illuminating dust motes that danced in the still air. Although she had been here many times, the space felt like it belonged to strangers. The couches, the neatly stacked books, and the meticulously dusted shelves all gave the impression of order, but a stifling, unspoken tension infused the air.

She had woken that morning with a dull ache behind her eyes and a shaky determination in her chest. Images of the drawings from under the floor were still seared into her mind. The frantic scribbles, the childlike scrawl, the face of a man she should not have been able to name as a little girl. And the letter from her mother, so stark and lacking in detail, now felt less like a confession and more like a calculated omission.

David Lewis, her father, stood near the window with

the uncertain posture of a man who sensed conflict but did not know how to contain it. He offered her an attempt at a reassuring smile, but the corners of his mouth twitched. On the coffee table sat a plate of untouched fruit and two cups of tea, already cooling.

Her mother, Anna Lewis, was in the adjacent dining room, methodically arranging mail. Ivy watched Anna's stillness, the rigid set of her shoulders, and felt the old pang of longing for a mother who would rush forward with comforting arms. Anna finally turned, and Ivy noticed the faint tremor in her hands, as if she dreaded this conversation. Yet there was a stubborn line across her brow that told Ivy no easy confessions would be coming.

The older woman pointed to a chair at the dining table. "Sit," she said, voice clipped. "We can talk in here."

The steps that carried Ivy across the threshold felt uncommonly loud. She slid into the chair, legs stiff and heartbeat drumming. A dullness settled in the house, broken only by David's footsteps as he came in behind them, taking a place near the head of the table. Anna took the seat across from Ivy, setting her palms flat on the table. The faint scent of her perfume, a clinical, almost antiseptic lavender, lingered. Ivy's attention was fixed on her mother's face.

A minute passed. The tension pressed against Ivy's chest, and she decided to speak first. She leaned forward, clasping her hands to stop them from trembling.

"Something's been gnawing at me all night," Ivy said. Her voice found a sharper edge. "Actually, for years now, if I'm being honest."

Anna did not blink. "I assumed as much the moment you phoned us," she said, cool but quiet. "I could tell you weren't dropping by to water the plants."

Ivy felt a bitter laugh rise. "No. I'm not here to take care of chores. I'm here because of what I found upstairs."

She paused long enough that her mother's fingers curled slightly against the table.

"Because, apparently, you already knew I was, different, when I was a child. You knew I had these visions, these urges to draw things beyond normal imagination." Her voice wavered. "And yet, you sealed it all away. You tried to hide it. You wrote a letter, left it with my drawings, then buried them under loose floorboards like they were something shameful."

Anna's mouth tightened. David stared at the table, lines of worry etched into his forehead. Finally, Anna cleared her throat.

"What would you have had me do, Ivy? You were six. You screamed at night about people burning, about impossible tragedies. If you had told that to anyone else, they would have labeled you psychotic. Or worse, they would have exploited your fantasies. I, your father and I, we didn't know how to help you. I tried to protect you from a world that would shred you if it found out you saw such things."

Ivy listened, and the excuse felt paper-thin, a partial truth designed to conceal a much larger one. Hiding drawings was one thing, but Ivy now knew it went so much deeper. The memory of the driftwood bench, the scent of sea salt, the weight of Mirielle's words. Her mother was omitting the most important part. She was omitting the journey, the plea for a cure, the choice to let a psychic stranger build walls inside her own daughter's mind.

"And you did more than just hide some drawings, didn't you, Mom?" Ivy's voice was dangerously quiet, cutting through Anna's careful defense. "Protect me from the world? Or protect me from myself? You took me somewhere. A commune on the coast, north of the city. To a seer."

The name hung in the air, unspoken but potent. Anna recoiled, her face a mask of disbelief. The blood drained from her cheeks, and her hands, which had been resting flat on the table, clenched into white-knuckled fists. David let out a small, sharp breath, looking from his wife to his daughter in pained silence.

"How..." Anna whispered, her composure finally shattering. "How could you possibly know that?"

"Because I went back," Ivy said, the words raw with a grief she was just beginning to understand. "I met the woman you asked to 'cure' me. She told me everything. She told me you begged her to stop my visions, and she refused. But she offered to shield me, to put up a psychic 'veil' so the nightmares wouldn't traumatize me anymore. She told you it was temporary. She told you to bring me back when I was older so I could learn control. But you never did. You saw that I was quiet, that I'd stopped drawing, and you took that as a cure. You let me forget, Mom. You let her wall off a part of my own mind."

"I did it to save you!" Anna cried, her voice cracking as she slammed a hand on the table. "You were disappearing!

You were a ghost in your own body, haunted by things no child should see. Yes, I took you there. We were desperate. And when she quieted the noise in your head, when you started smiling again, when you were finally *my daughter* again... I couldn't risk losing you back to that darkness. It was a choice I made for you, for your sanity."

Ivy felt her jaw clench. "But you didn't protect me. You erased me. Those drawings were mine. That letter was so clinical, so empty of details. As if you were wiping a chalkboard, trying to start fresh. But you can't wipe a person. Those things I saw still happened inside my head, whether I remembered them or not."

Anna's eyes glinted with an emotion Ivy could not decipher. "Perhaps I went about it the wrong way, but it was never my intention to harm you," Anna said. "I only wanted to dull the nightmares."

Ivy sat back against the dining chair. She closed her eyes for a moment, summoning the courage to say her words. She no longer wanted to carry the burden of uncertainty alone. She opened her eyes and fixed her gaze on her mother once more.

"You tried to erase me," Ivy repeated, voice low. "Not protect me, erase me."

Anna's lips parted, as if to deny it, but no denial came. "You were six and screaming about people dying," she whispered, "and it was constant. I couldn't sleep. I could barely function. You were... tormented. What was I supposed to do, Ivy? Let you grow up haunted?"

The question hung in the air, jagged and raw. Ivy's eyes stung with tears she refused to shed. She remembered fleeting moments of her mother's alarmed face, the dismissive tones. All those memories condensed into one suffocating truth. Her mother had always been afraid of her gift.

"I grew up haunted anyway," Ivy whispered, glancing at her father. He seemed pained, but he did not speak. She refocused on Anna. "You can't bury something that's part of me. You can't sweep it under the floor and pretend it's never going to resurface. It did, and now I'm left to handle it on my own."

Anna's calm mask slipped, revealing a glimmer of regret in her dark eyes. "I didn't believe you could manage it," she said softly. "Not even when you were older. And I..." Her voice cut off as she glanced away, hands twisting in her lap. "I was worried about how the rest of the world would handle it, too."

Ivy's heartbeat thundered. For years, she had wanted some sign from her mother that she understood. But hearing Anna's confession now only fueled Ivy's sense that they had wasted so much time in silence and denial.

"You never asked me how I felt," Ivy fought the tremor in her voice. "You decided for me. You wrote that letter and tucked it beneath those boards as though you were burying a corpse. Like you were ashamed."

Anna expelled a slow, uneven breath. "I thought that by hiding those pictures, the drawings of disasters and strangers you had no way of knowing, I could spare you a life under a microscope. I was under the impression that if you forgot, you'd grow up normal. I didn't want you labeled as a misfit. You were my child. I had to do something."

Ivy pinched the bridge of her nose. "And in doing so, you made me believe that everything out of the ordinary was a disease to be cured. I spent years ashamed of every intuition, every strange dream, thinking you'd lock me up if I told you. Do you realize how isolating that felt?" The words tumbled out, raw and honest. "You changed the locks on my own mind, Mother. I've spent half my life convinced I was broken."

David, who had been silent, cleared his throat. "Anna," he interrupted softly, "If you would only..."

Ivy caught his gaze and shook her head. She wanted no one to smooth this over. She returned her focus to her mother.

"I never intended you to feel broken," Anna professed, voice trembling. "I meant only to shield you. Now... I see maybe I misunderstood what shielding meant."

Ivy could have pointed out the times she had awakened from a nightmare only to be greeted by Anna's forced smile or scolding. But her anger mingled with sorrow.

"Did you ever regret it?" Ivy asked quietly. "Hiding my drawings, hiding my truth, did you once think that revealing them might help me find answers?"

Anna blinked back tears. "I was afraid," she whispered. "Afraid of losing you as I lost my..." She stopped and pressed her lips together. "We have a family history of traits we never spoke about, and I... I handled it poorly."

Ivy felt her pulse skip. She wondered if her mother was alluding to the grandmother who also saw visions, or to

Aunt Cassandra. But Anna's words dried up. A wave of frustration coursed through Ivy. Even now, Anna refused to fully open the locked door.

"That's enough," Ivy's voice was soft yet firm. "I understand that you felt you had no choice. But that doesn't change the fact that you hurt me more by hiding the truth."

David opened his mouth to speak again, but Ivy lifted a hand. She braced herself for the final step of this conversation. Her heart drummed against her ribs, fueled by the knowledge that she could no longer tiptoe around who she was.

"You wrote in that letter that you hoped I would understand," she said, swallowing hard. "Maybe I do, a little. I understand fear. But I don't accept the way you handled it. There is a difference. And I won't let that fear dictate my life anymore."

Anna closed her eyes, tears wet on her lashes. Shadows under them betrayed sleepless nights. David sat very still, his eyes darting from Ivy's face to Anna's trembling shoulders. Ivy paused, gathering her strength. If she backed down now, she feared she might unravel her progress. She inhaled deeply, letting the quiet drag out until the tension felt almost physical.

She stood, her chair scraping against the floor. She glanced from Anna to David, feeling a pang of sympathy for her father's desperation to keep the family intact. But she could not let that sympathy erase all that had been lost. A trembling in her limbs reminded her of her own anger, but she steadied herself.

In a voice that resonated across the silent dining room, she spoke the words she had come here to speak, the words that would set her free.

"I'm not asking for an apology," she announced, letting each syllable carry the weight of her conviction.

She felt David draw in a sharp breath, saw Anna's gaze drop to the table.

"I'm telling you, I'm not hiding anymore."

TWENTY-SIX

THE SEER'S WAKE

Night settled over San Francisco with an eerie tranquility. A thin veil of fog wove past the street-lamps, rounding the corners of Dolores Park with pale fingers of light. Ivy stood at the edge of the grass, phone clutched in her hand, watching the glow of hundreds of candles glinting across the wide lawn. Too many people to count had gathered. Some formed small circles, quietly speaking. Others stood alone in stoic silence. The air smelled faintly of melted wax and damp earth.

She had not planned to leave her apartment that night. For days following her clash with her parents, she had felt restless. Sleep offered little comfort, laced with half-formed visions of shadows moving through narrow corridors. Yet something about the low hum of voices and the glow of candlelight outside Dolores Park tugged her from her gloom. She had looked out the window, seen the gimmers in the distance, and felt that unmistakable pull in her gut.

Her phone buzzed. She glanced down at Ethan's name. They had texted only moments ago. She had asked him, "What's going on in the park?"

He replied, "I'm not sure. Some kind of public vigil. I'll meet you soon."

A slow chill prickled at her neck. She could not tell if it was the breeze or the inkling that this vigil was not what it seemed. In the distance, two men in dark jackets approached the candlelit area, heads bowed. A quiet fell over the crowd, and other figures drifted closer as if guided by some silent signal.

Ivy slid her phone into her cardigan pocket and stepped onto the grass, weaving between clusters of mourners. She glimpsed small altars. Framed photographs, scattered flowers, tiny plates of offerings. She wondered whom they honored. But something suggested a deeper significance.

She moved farther along and noticed a small dais at the center of the park. Men and women stood in irregular rows. A faint chant rose and fell. The words were soft and unintelligible. Ivy caught a glimpse of a tear rolling down someone's cheek, reflecting the flame of a candle they held.

In her chest, that familiar tension curled tighter. She glanced over her shoulder. No sign of Ethan yet. She almost wanted to call him again, but the pressing sensation in her ribs compelled her to keep moving. The grass underfoot was soft from recent drizzle. The fog caught the light of a candle's flame, sparkling briefly.

A figure in a hooded cloak glided past, the fabric

skimming the grass. Ivy's pulse kicked. The cloak reminded her of the nerve-racking illusions she had once seen. She swallowed her anxiety and followed at a careful distance. The hooded person stopped near a weathered statue in the park's center. Candles crowded the statue's base. Their flames threw dancing shapes against the worn stone. Ivy went around a knot of bystanders to get a clearer view. Her phone vibrated once more, but she ignored it. Her attention locked on the hooded figure. The person turned, as if sensing her stare. At first, she only saw the outline of a jaw beneath the hood's edge. He took two steps toward her and candlelight lit his face. The man stared at her with milky white eyes. No iris or pupil. Just an unsettling wash of pale color.

Her breath caught. The man seemed to pinpoint her location perfectly. His expression twisted, as though he recognized her. He reached out, fingers closing around her wrist with surprising strength. An alarmed gasp escaped her lips. The world around them seemed to recede.

"You are not the first," the man whispered. His voice trembled and cracked, yet it carried a force that felt far older than his frail body. "You are not... the last."

Ivy's stomach knotted. She opened her mouth, but no words came out. His grip tightened, and she felt his nails biting into her skin through the sleeve of her cardigan. The faint smell of burnt sage clung to him.

He repeated his words, louder this time. "You are not the first. And you are not the last." Then his body jolted. His eyes rolled back. His grip slackened, and he dropped to the ground at her feet. His candle tumbled and sputtered out.

For a single second, Ivy went numb. She stared at the man sprawled on the grass. His hood fell backward, revealing wispy gray hair and a face etched with deep lines. Strangled murmurs rose from the people around them. Shock darted like a current through the crowd. Someone shouted, and in the next instant, everything broke into chaos.

"Call an ambulance," a woman cried, panic cracking her voice.

Ivy dropped to her knees beside him, ignoring the damp that soaked into her jeans. She pressed shaking fingers to the side of his neck, desperate to find a pulse. Her own heartbeat thudded so loudly it drowned out the rustle of the crowd. No hint of life responded. His jaw had slackened, lips parted.

Her mind spun. She barely registered the hands of strangers reaching to help. The lights from cell phones grew to a harsh glare.

Someone grasped her arm. She lifted her head. Ethan stood over her, breath ragged, eyes filled with concern. He helped her to her feet, pulling her away from the growing commotion. Nearby, a few individuals bent over the lifeless stranger, pressing on his chest in a futile attempt at CPR. The rhythmic chant from the beginning of the vigil fractured into panicked shouts.

"Are you hurt?" Ethan asked, searching her face. "What happened?"

Ivy struggled to respond. "I'm... not hurt, but that

man…" She stopped. "He said something to me. Told me I wasn't the first or the last."

Ethan's brows drew tight. "I'm going to call for help." He patted his jacket pockets, but the faint knell of sirens already drifted through the park.

Around them, a few people drifted away, frightened by the sudden death in their midst. Others stood rooted to the spot. Candles toppled, snuffed out in the crush of moving feet. The entire vigil disintegrated into confusion. Ivy tried not to look at the body, but her gaze kept wandering back. Guilt burrowed under her skin, although she had no rational cause for it. The man's words replayed in her mind. Her thoughts rushed to her old drawings and the weird sense of inevitability she had felt upon discovering them.

"Stay with me, okay?" Ethan rested his hand gently on her shoulder.

She nodded. But on the periphery of her vision, she noticed a familiar item in Ethan's other hand. A sealed envelope. Her pulse lurched. It was exactly like the cream-colored envelope that had appeared once before.

"I found this taped to your shop's door," his voice was quiet. "No return address. I recognized the seal. The same bull's-eye imprint. I opened it."

He hesitated, scanning her face. Her fear spiked again. The hooded man's death, these repeated messages, everything rippled outward. The distant wail of a siren cut through the confusion as several paramedics hustled across the park. Ivy moved to one side. Over the paramedics' urgent activity, Ethan maneuvered Ivy away, guiding her past watchers. He got her into a darker patch under an old oak tree.

He held up the envelope once more. Then he unfolded a slip of paper from inside. The shaky candlelight from the vigil illuminated bold, handwritten letters. Ethan read it out loud in a near-whisper, his voice vibrating with disbelief. "To Lucien Grey. She has begun."

At those words, Ivy's entire body went rigid. The name struck at her with lightning intensity. Lucien Grey was the man in her visions, the man whose face she had scrawled in charcoal as a child.

Fear and an odd undercurrent of awareness twisted in her gut. Her mind raced back to the portrait she had found. Lucien's eyes seemed to peer at her from memory, half-lidded with that faint, mocking smile. She struggled to remain upright. Ethan's arm steadied her. She blinked, forcing herself to focus. People hurried in the background, shouts blending with the ambulance siren that grew louder as it approached. The air smelled of hot wax, burnt wick, and a faint leftover tang of incense. She felt the thick pounding of her heart as every muscle in her body coiled in alarm.

Whispers from the edges of her senses nagged at her; a premonition or simply shock from the man's death. She heard the words again, told by that milky-eyed stranger. *You are not the first. And you are not the last.* She rubbed her wrist where he had grabbed her. Her skin felt electrified, as though something potent had passed from him to her.

Ethan's hand brushed her shoulder again. "Ivy. That name, Lucien Grey, didn't you..."

"Yes," she managed. Her voice sounded husky to her own ears. "He's the... I saw him in old drawings. I kept dreaming about him. Aunt Cassandra mentioned him, though never with clarity."

Ethan's expression tightened. "Whoever left this envelope thinks that message belongs to him. They're announcing something... like an event, or an awakening."

Ivy glanced at the lifeless shape on the grass, half-shielded by the paramedics, and swallowed. She knew her presence in the park tonight had not been random. It was all braided into the same tapestry. One thread twisted into the next. Now a man was dead at her feet, whispering cryptic clues with his final breath, while an envelope spelled out a name that haunted her nights.

Her teeth grazed her lower lip. The edges of her eyes stung with unshed tears. She did not want to cry. She wanted answers. How this was tied to her, how Lucien factored into it, and why it felt as though the entire city balanced on a precarious brink.

Ethan read the line once more, quieter. "To Lucien Grey. She has begun."

Ivy exhaled a trembling breath. Her mind raced, conjuring the memory of Lucien's face from the old drawing. She pictured his sharp features, the cunning arch of his brows. Alarm pulsed in her bloodstream. He was not simply a name on paper or a vague memory. He was real, and somehow a letter directly referencing him had arrived at her door.

Ivy's stomach knotted with realization. The man from her dreams, the man she had drawn in a childlike scrawl, was more than a distant phantom. He was waiting for her. A chill traced every inch of her spine. She met Ethan's gaze, hoping to find steady ground. Yet in that moment, all she could do was let the truth crash over her in one terrifying surge.

Lucien Grey was here, somewhere, weaving threads of a plan she scarcely understood. She wanted to believe she could run from this, but she already knew the truth. She had begun, and there would be no turning back.

THE STORY CONTINUES

The story continues in book two, **DARK DREAMS,** coming soon to Amazon.

EXCERPT FROM DARK DREAMS

CHAPTER ONE

Ivy felt her pulse roaring in her ears as the paramedics rushed forward, flooding the candlelit darkness with strobing red and blue. The hooded man lay on his side in the grass, face turned away from the glow of the street-lamps. His tangled gray hair fanned around him like a halo. A pair of mourners stumbled back, giving the medics space. Ivy watched them kneel beside the body and begin CPR, but it was clear to anyone nearby that the man was gone.

She still felt the echo of his grip around her wrist, a phantom pressure that refused to leave her skin. His eyes had been milky and pale, as though he had stared into a world no one else could see. *You are not the first... and you are not the last.* She could still hear that rasping voice, so frail yet oddly forceful.

Ethan touched her shoulder gently. "Come on," he said in a low tone. "You're freezing out here."

Everything around them blurred, the sorrowful silence

of onlookers blending with the pulsing lights and the steady drone of sirens. Ivy nodded, unable to form words yet. She let Ethan guide her away from the wavering candles and the circle of stiff-lipped paramedics still trying and failing to bring the stranger back.

He led her across the street to a small cafe whose interior glimmered with string lights in the windows. A chalkboard sign out front promised espresso and fresh pastries, though it was well past the dinner hour. Ivy sank into one of the wooden chairs by the window, her gaze drifting to where the vigil still glowed in Dolores Park. The distance offered no comfort. She kept expecting the man to rise, to appear once more in that hood, telling her cryptic truths she could not decipher.

Ethan slid into the seat across from her. He hesitated before offering a hand, which she took. The warmth of his fingers wrapped around hers, grounding her. She tried to focus on the mundane details around them, the scuffed table, the overhead lights humming softly, the smell of roasted coffee beans. Ordinary anchors in a night riddled with shock.

A waitress approached, her face lined with worry. "You two all right?" she asked, her voice stifled as though she sensed something amiss.

Ethan nodded. "Just coffee, please." He glanced at Ivy, who managed a small nod. "Make it two," he added.

The waitress slid away to fill their order, leaving them in a silence interrupted only by the chatter of a few customers who looked too tired to care about the flurry of activity outside. Ivy swallowed tightly.

"He recognized me," she said at last. Her voice sounded distant, like it belonged to someone else. "The way he grabbed my wrist, it was so deliberate. Like he'd been waiting for me."

Ethan's eyes rested on her face. "What did he say exactly?"

Her throat constricted. She forced the words out. *That I'm not the first, and I'm not the last.* The memory sent a ripple of unease through her body. "It felt like a warning."

He gently squeezed her hand, then reached into his jacket pocket. Out came a cream-colored envelope sealed with wax. Ivy stared at it, recalling the chill that swept through her when he first showed it to her in the park. The same archaic seal, the same thick paper, the same sense of looming mystery.

Ethan's voice dropped low. "I opened this while I was looking for you. Inside is that name again." He leaned forward, lowering his voice. "*Lucien Grey.*"

The name spilled onto the worn tabletop like a living thing. Ivy inhaled sharply. She had seen it scrawled beneath that strange charcoal portrait hidden under her parents' floorboards. Lucien Grey had haunted her sketches as a child, a name she should never have known so young. Now it surfaced again, linked to a dead man's last words.

Ethan lifted the envelope and slid it across to her, letting her see the handwritten scrawl. He traced one finger over the lines of ink. "Do you know him?" he asked softly, studying her eyes.

Ivy barely breathed. She remembered the face she had

once etched, the angular cheekbones and half-smiling mouth she couldn't possibly have imagined at age six. Her pulse lurched. "Only from dreams," she whispered. "Until recently, I thought maybe I made him up. Maybe it was just some childhood nightmare." She inhaled a trembling breath. "I don't think it's pretend anymore."

The coffees arrived with quiet efficiency. The waitress set them down and slipped away again, her eyes darting with mild curiosity toward the envelope. Neither Ivy nor Ethan touched the mugs, their focus firmly on the unsettling message.

Ethan flipped open his laptop. He kept it tucked in his messenger bag everywhere he went, always prepared to chase a lead. Tonight, the bag sat slung over the back of his chair, the laptop balanced on his knees.

"Let's see if Lucien Grey actually exists," he murmured.

They searched local records first. Nothing. Then they widened the search to broader public databases, scanning for any mention of Lucien Grey in real estate transactions, obituaries, or business holdings. The results turned up scattered references but nothing that felt concrete. There was a Lucien Grey in London from decades ago, tied to an abandoned estate. Another mention of the name appeared in a genealogical site listing births from the 1890s. Each record was old, the location far away from present-day San Francisco. No current addresses popped up, no official presence.

"Strange," Ethan muttered, tapping the trackpad. "Without a birth date or a location, we can't confirm if it's the same person. He might just be a name repeated over different centuries, or it could be one man using an alias." His voice trailed off.

A chill crept along Ivy's spine. The wavering images of her childhood drawings floated in her memory. She'd scrawled the same face, the same name again and again, like an obsession that she didn't understand. She rubbed her arms, trying to ward off the cold sinking into her chest.

Ethan scrolled through digital archives. Some writings dated back to the early twentieth century, citing a mysterious figure rumored to be a spiritualist in Europe. Then in the 1950s, another rumor surfaced in old, unverified newspaper clippings about a Lucien Grey leading secret gatherings in North America. The language was half gossip, half cautionary tale.

"This is like chasing a ghost," Ethan said. "He doesn't stay in one place long, and none of these accounts prove he's the same person. Could be a family line or a string of impostors." He closed the laptop gently, letting out a tense breath. "But that doesn't explain why his name keeps following you."

Ivy could only shake her head, her gaze drifting to the vigil site across the street. The bright clusters of candles in Dolores Park still danced in the darkness. The quiet of that place clung to her, as though the dead man's final warning hovered in the air. She shivered.

Ethan reached for her hand again. The heat of his palm steadied her, reminding her that she was not alone in this. He angled his head, lowering his voice. "We will figure it out," he said. "Whoever Lucien Grey is, we'll find something eventually."

She wanted to believe that. She wanted to believe they could unravel this mystery with enough research and stubborn resolve. Yet a part of her knew the truth wove itself through deeper layers, through visions and half-forgotten childhood memories, through the glimpses of nightmares that sometimes felt too real. They finished their coffees in weighted silence, neither quite ready to lay out every fear on the table. When the waitress returned with the check, Ivy noticed the quiver in her own fingers. Her reflection in the cafe's tinted window revealed a woman who looked rattled, her eyes shadowed, her mouth pressed thin. She forced a small nod of thanks at the waitress, grateful for the warm interior even if it did little to calm her mind.

Outside, the cold air stung her cheeks. The vigil had thinned somewhat, people departing as the authorities stepped in. Ivy and Ethan walked in subdued quiet back to where he'd parked. Another ambulance cruised by, lights spinning. Ivy's lungs felt tight, as if the night's events pressed inward. She wanted to ask Ethan to stay with her, not for overt romance, but simply because the thought of being alone in her apartment felt too heavy to bear.

He seemed to sense her unspoken plea. Even as he unlocked the car, he gave her a measured look. "We can go to your place," he said quietly. "I'll stay long enough to make sure you're okay. Let you settle in. You shouldn't be alone."

Ivy exhaled an unsteady breath and nodded. She

noticed the tension in his posture, the soft look of concern in his eyes. He took it seriously, her rattled devotion to these visions and to the dead man's words. The city lights blurred past as they drove, neither of them speaking much, the hum of the engine filling the silence with a low vibration that mirrored the uneasy flutter in her gut.

When they reached her building, Ivy climbed out, wincing at the drizzle that had started to fall. They hurried upstairs to her apartment. Inside, she flipped on a single lamp, revealing the quiet warmth of her small living space. Books lay scattered across the coffee table, alongside a half-burned candle that had collected a pool of wax.

Ethan set his laptop on the couch. "You need anything?"

She shook her head. "I just need to breathe." She peeled off her coat and shoes, rubbing her arms as she moved to the kitchen for a glass of water. The normality of the routine calmed her somewhat. The water glinted in the yellowish overhead light when she took a sip.

Ethan waited, leaning against the arm of the couch, arms folded lightly. He looked ready to drop if she asked him to leave, but her chest tightened at the thought of him going. She walked over and sank onto the sofa. "Stay for a little while," she said, her voice stifled. "I'm not sure I can sleep after tonight."

His shoulders softened. He sat and reached tentatively for her hand. She let him hold it, allowing that connection to ease the knots in her stomach. For a long moment, they stayed like that, side by side on the couch, the lamp casting warm shadows around them. Outside, the drizzle grew into a faint tap against the windows.

Ivy felt exhaustion sweep through her like a current. She tried to fight it, but her eyes kept drooping shut. She was vaguely aware of Ethan standing, retrieving a blanket from a chair, and draping it over her shoulders. She mumbled a protest, but the weight of the night crushed her attempts at alertness.

"Get some rest," he said softly, his breath warm against her temple. She nodded, drifting in and out of a shallow doze. Though she did not fully remember him leaving, she thought she heard the soft click of the door eventually. Perhaps he lingered in the hallway a moment before disappearing into the misty night.

At some indeterminate point later, Ivy glimpsed herself standing in a desolate place. The dream formed around her like smoke. A glance revealed cracked pews, the overhead arches of an abandoned church. Moonlight, cold and silvery, filtered through broken stained-glass windows. Vines crept up the walls, twisted and thick, as if the building had been left to rot in some forgotten quarter of the city.

"Ivy," a voice called. It flowed from the shadows, low and eerie. She scanned the darkness between the stone columns. There, a figure stepped into a narrow shaft of moonlight. He wore a dark coat, slender and pristine, and his eyes gleamed as if they held mirrors. His face was painfully familiar, the same face she had once sketched so many times, the face she had convinced herself was a relic of her childhood nightmares.

She tried to speak, but her voice caught. A wave of cold dread spread through her. He moved closer, the silence stretching, until she could see the faint curve of his mouth as if he might smile.

I've been watching, he said softly. His voice threaded the air like silk, each word infused with quiet certainty. *You feel it, don't you?*

Ivy's heart pounded. She wanted to back away, but her body stayed rooted in place, as though compelled by some invisible force. In one wavering instant, she realized his presence in her visions had never gone away. He had always been there, shimmering in the corners of dreamscapes she refused to remember. Her lips parted, but no sound emerged.

He stepped forward again, close enough that she could see a faint luminous quality on his skin, something almost ageless. His gaze turned to her hands. *You found my name,* he said, an undercurrent of amusement in his tone. *And soon, you will need me.*

Despair threatened to crush her chest. She wanted to wake up, to tear herself free. She summoned all her will and pushed against the stagnant air of the church, struggling like someone pinned by an impossible weight.

The dream shattered.

Ivy jolted upright in her apartment, gasping for breath. Her nightshirt clung to her damp skin as if she had run a marathon. Moonlight probed through the window, revealing the empty living room. The blanket had slid off her shoulders. She placed a trembling hand over her heartbeat, trying to quiet the frantic rhythm. The echo of Lucien's words, *I've been watching*, pounded in her mind.

She pressed her back against the couch cushions, pulse racing, grappling with the renewed terror that he was not just some obscure name in a half-buried letter. He was real. His presence clung to her like a shadow, and her heart hammered as if trying to escape her ribs.

Outside, the rain tapped persistently, and the city slept on, unaware. Ivy swallowed a trembling breath, tears burning at the corners of her eyes. She could not stop the flood of dread that insisted Lucien was closer than ever before.

She stared at the faint reflection of her wide-eyed face in the dark window. For a moment, she thought she saw a second silhouette standing behind her. Then the image dissolved into the night. She was alone, heart pounding, with no answers and a new terror settling in her veins.

OTHER FLORID ROMANCE BOOKS

To be notified of new releases and special promotions from Florid Romance, please join our email list:

https://floridromance.lmbpn.com/about/sign-up-for-our-newsletter/

For a complete list of books published by Florid Romance please visit our website:

https://floridromance.lmbpn.com/

BOOKS BY KELLI ROBYNS

The Enchanted Orchard

The Orchard (Book 1)

Family Curse (Book 2)

Crystal Heart (Book 3)

The Charmed City

Spellbound (Book 1)

Prophecy (Book 2)

Ultimatum (Book 3)

Crescent City Curse

Beignets and Bad Omens (Book 1)

Moonlight and Muddy Waters (Book 2)

Queen of the Quarter (Book 3)

In My Mind's Eye

Oracle Project (Book 1)

Dark Dreams (Book 2)

BOOKS BY MICHAEL ANDERLE

Sign up for the **LMBPN** email list to be notified of new releases and special deals!

https://lmbpn.com/email/

For a complete list of books by Michael Anderle, please visit:

www.lmbpn.com/ma-books/

CONNECT WITH MICHAEL ANDERLE

Website: http://lmbpn.com

Email List: https://michael.beehiiv.com/

https://www.facebook.com/LMBPNPublishing

https://twitter.com/MichaelAnderle

https://www.instagram.com/lmbpn_publishing/

https://www.bookbub.com/authors/michael-anderle